City of Kingz 2

Chris Green

Lock Down Publications and Ca$h
Presents
City of Kingz 2
A Novel by *Chris Green*

Lock Down Publications
P.O. Box 944
Stockbridge, Ga 30281

Visit our website @
www.lockdownpublications.com

Copyright 2021 by Chris Green
City of Kingz 2

Lock Down Publications
Like our page on Facebook: Lock Down Publications @
www.facebook.com/lockdownpublications.ldp
Cover design and layout by: **Dynasty Cover Me**
Book interior design by: **Shawn Walker**
Edited by: **Shamika Smith**

Chris Green

Stay Connected with Us!

Text **LOCKDOWN** to 22828 to stay up-to-date with new releases, sneak peaks, contests and more…
Thank you.

Submission Guideline.

Submit the first three chapters of your completed manuscript to ldpsubmissions@gmail.com, subject line: Your book's title. The manuscript must be in a .doc file and sent as an attachment. Document should be in Times New Roman, double spaced and in size 12 font. Also, provide your synopsis and full contact information. If sending multiple submissions, they must each be in a separate email.

Have a story but no way to send it electronically? You can still submit to LDP/Ca$h Presents. Send in the first three chapters, written or typed, of your completed manuscript to:

LDP: Submissions Dept
P.O. Box 944
Stockbridge, Ga 30281

DO NOT send original manuscript. Must be a duplicate.

Provide your synopsis and a cover letter containing your full contact information.

Thanks for considering LDP and Ca$h Presents.

Chris Green

Acknowledgements

Black love is a valuable, and sensitive subject that's going on in the world today. Right now, in the year 2020, the black race has received more separation losses than any other race in the United States. We have been slain by our own people. The law. The opposition of our skin color, and numerous of individuals who aren't even aware of the reason they're taking a life. Since my last book, I have lost so much: family, friends, ideas, finances, and ways that I never realized was harming myself.

I, Author Chris Green, has risen to a new level with my mind frame. A new attitude for my path of success. And a strategic way to have a second thought process before I react to my first thought. Patience is a major key to winning when it comes to anything, and I still have a lot to build, and grow upon inside this strange, but unique world. We were all based with one similarity, and that was free will to do as we pleased. My take on that is to begin doing what I need instead, before entertaining things I want. I'm growing. Not only for myself, but also for the ones who aren't able to have the courage like me to let go. The negativity lives deeply in certain unappreciative humans, and their polluted actions of being so miserable could wrap your brain tighter than an ace bandage until it squeezes the life clean from your pores like a fresh orange from our grandmother's cold refrigerator.

The message of this means try and watch how much of your time you allow to be engaged in fruitless mixtures. If the pitcher can't be sweetened for you to build and grow like the strongest tree in the rain forest, cut it up from the roots, and try to focus on how to correctly water your seed in order to sprout a true foundation for life. You are success. You are books. WeRBooks, We are LDP, and we are creation. Never forget your way of physical, mental, a spiritual growth. Those three branches together connect the lines to

6

your heart in order to beat accordingly. Once that coordination is tampered with. Your life slowly decreases until the limbs falls off, and destroy you completely. I love you guys. All my readers are my WORLD! Your love is amazing, and I promise my pen will slide, and puzzle words together until you all feel that the torch is ready to be passed. Peace and Love always and forever. Splitting my heart for a portion of negativity. I'm sorry. I could never.

Dedication

First as always, The creator Allah (swt) My daughter Cerenity Green. My mother, Dolsellia Green. My twin and brother, Deangelo Green. My uncle, sister, Grandmas, aunties, and cousins. Y'all are Greens which means I have a fulfillment to meet. Shout out to my Osa Traditional associated businesses, and Brothers of the company. Our brand is critiquing daily. We just have to keep faith that our Grind will shine. My brother Saint (Cornelius Mouton) Marquise Rice (Hamza) Jerrell Thompson (Abdul Qawi) Many more that I can't spill so soon because I'm not rushing to see if the next few will remain loyal. It's a part of my growth. Let this great, and suspenseful novel take you on a journey to see how talented I have truly worked to become.

Chris Green

Chapter 1
3:45 A.M.

As Keyno stepped out of the bank, the sun pierced his skin. The sound of the loud police sirens could be heard as they began to pour out of the intersecting streets behind him. He wasted no time firing six shots to let them know that going back to prison wasn't an option.

Boc! Boc! Boc! Boc! Boc! Boc!

He could see Jabari and Sip's getaway car posted on the opposite side of the street, but the Sacramento Police were now spilling from every back area killing any hope for running in a different direction. His chest was heaving hard, and he could feel the force gaining down on him with every step he took.

Blow took his chances running across the street in front of the flying vehicles. Before Keyno could dash behind him, a barrage of shots began to ring out loudly. The bullet that pierced his leg forced him to cringe and crumble to the ground. "Fuckk!"

Jabari was standing by the driver's side of the whip when he witnessed his friend hit the ground. Aiming his weapon at the group of police, he let off ten rapid shots forcing them to take cover behind their cruisers.

Pak! Pak! Pak! Pak! Pak! Pak! Pak! Pakkk!

The semi-automatic burped loudly.

"Get up Keyno! You gotta get up!" Jabari cried out.

He struggled to stand from the gun wound and slid back to the ground. The police cars were now blocking off the small area and trying to move slowly towards him. "Just go lil bro!" he shouted, realizing that the car was too far for him to make it.

Jabari continued to pop his gun forcing the cops to retreat back behind their vehicles. Blow's driver, Sip, wasted no time smashing off once he got inside the passenger side of his car, leaving the team to fight against the authorities of the law alone. "Keyno, get up. Please! You gotta stand up big bro."

Struggling to absorb the pain in his leg, he tried to move again. The time seemed to freeze in slow motion when one of the officers raised up with his twelve-gauge shotgun, pulling the trigger. The large slug slammed into Keyno's back sending a chunk flying from his stomach.

BOOM!

"Nooooo!" Jabari screamed when the shot was released from the officer's weapon.

Keyno covered the hole in his body slowly. He mustered up enough energy to look in Jabari's eyes. "Tell mama that I love her, bro," he mumbled before crashing face-first into the concrete.

Jumping up from his sleep, Jabari's face was pouring sweat profusely. His chest heaved up and down, and he wasted no time reaching for the pistol that rested under his pillow. Victoria raised up placing her soft hand against his chest.

"Baby calm down. It's just another bad dream. Calm down Jabari," she whispered, kissing his cheek repeatedly.

The small wind from his balcony window blew heavily causing a light chill to flow through his body. The thought of seeing Keyno in his dream for the fifth time was sitting so crooked in his mind. He couldn't sleep for days, and now the guiltiness of leaving his friend behind was haunting him with every night that passed by.

Victoria grabbed the cold glass of water from their nightstand forcing him to drink it. Taking large sips until the cup was empty, he lowered his head and laid against her shoulder. "I can't stop dreaming about him."

Victoria held his shoulder before rubbing a hand through his soft waves. "Was it like the last few dreams?"

"No…He…he said something to me before he died. It felt like I was reliving the same moment again," Jabari huffed and closed his eyes.

Looking at him with a confused face, Victoria sat up. "What did he say?"

Jabari paused for a slight second before answering, "He said tell mama that I love her."

Hearing the statement caused Victoria's mind to ponder, but she refused to make him more uncomfortable with his problem at the moment. Kissing his lips passionately, she pulled him back down next to her on their king-size bed. "You need rest baby. Just try and think of something else to get you through the night. It's gonna be okay," she pleaded with sincerity in her eyes.

Nodding silently, he cuddled back up next to her. However, the fear of another dream forced him to keep his eyes open. He never experienced something that felt so real. It was like Keyno's words moved through his soul. Taking a deep breath, he prayed in his mind that rest could ease his pain, and the torment could be snatched from his heart. The evil deeds were trying to send a message his way, and he didn't know why. Something wasn't sitting right, and Jabari knew he wouldn't stop until he found out the reason. Even if that meant him placing his own life on the line. Placing a hand on Keyno's dog tag that rested around his neck, he mumbled to himself, "Don't second guess me, Keyno. I trust you."

* * *

Sacramento Police Department
Detective Pakori's Investigation Unit

As Detective Pakori scrolled down the large file that sat on his computer screen. He clicked on numerous different mugshots of

11

criminals who were arrested in the past ten years for armed robberies and released. The crime rate in California was rising daily, and over the past year, there had been more than twelve banks smashed by a group of filthy scumbags who had yet to be taken down. It was hard to build a case on a bunch of ghosts. Numerous crime-stopper calls were made, and still, there was no justice that could be served on the city of Sacramento for the citizens' hard-earned savings.

The knocking on his office door forced him to break his attention from the screen for a second. "Come in."

The woman who stepped inside wore her rusty red hair in a large ponytail. Her olive skin boomed with a small tan adding more compliments to her amazing shape. Her eyes were light sky blue and could easily make you believe that she was an underworld vampire from the white crystals that danced in her pupils. She was a doll in human form, not to mention one of the best detectives on Sacramento's Marksman Shooting Force.

Her name was Shannon Kegg, and besides being one of the most respected women in the unit, her father was FBI Agent Patrick Kegg. He made sure that his princess didn't have to answer to anyone when it came down to the way she operated her authority. Graduating from Yale University with outstanding dual degrees in Sociology, Biology, Forensic Science, and a Juris Doctor of Law degree. Her name rang bells over the average people in school who flaunted their money and skills for trades that didn't hold weight for a damn thing. After spending four years in the Marines, she acquired every medal possible for shooting a handgun, assault rifle, and even using a battle knife. Retiring back home to the Sacramento police force she earned the name G.I Jane.

Taking a seat in the chair at Detective Pakori's desk, she crossed her leg. "Good morning, sir."

"Morning Shannon. You're looking extra presentable today. I can see the fuckery written all over your face. What's on your mind?" Pakori asked, leaning back in his chair.

"Banks," she replied dryly, cocking her neck to the side.

Pakori huffed and leaned back in his chair. "How did I feel this had to be something of that nature? I'm listening."

"Well, it seems to me that all the males are slipping like Crisco in the station. For the past year, I've sat back investigating murder after murder. And quite frankly, I'm tired, Pakori. If it's possible, I would like to get in on the bank robbery cases for Sacramento. I've been doing my own research, and I may have something," she said with confidence.

"Shannon these cases are confidential, and you need a higher authority in order to go tapping around with things like this."

"Pakori, my father is enough authority, and you love me because you know that I can get the job done. I'm requesting a shot, but I'm not asking."

Forcing a smile on his face, Pakori shook his head. "You can't just buck on everyone, Shannon. I am still your boss, you know."

"Yes, sir. I know." She grinned, opening her small file. "Last year around September 18th, the WestAmerica Bank on 1610 Arden Way. It was robbed by four men. Three gunmen, and one driver. Over seventy-five grand was taken and these guys were out of that area in less than one hundred and twenty seconds. The next bank was Merchants National Bank on 1015 7th'st.It's mostly a credit union which means that it holds more money. It was exactly one hundred and forty thousand dollars taken, and these guys were only in the establishment for forty-five seconds. That's seventy-five seconds lesser than the first robbery, which proves that these guys were doing a lot of homework. There was only one difference this time. There were five of them. Four gunmen, and one driver.

These same steps were followed for the next five banks along the Sacramento's county line."

Detective Pakori was now listening with all ears as Shannon poured him a cup of knowledge about his confidential case. Not only was her theory adding up, but there were things that she wasn't supposed to know spilling from between her lips. Pakori waved his hand gesturing for her to continue.

"Now that I've gathered the small info from all the following robberies. I fast-forwarded a year later to the River's City B. That bank hadn't been robbed in over sixteen years. It was actually one of the most protected establishments inside of Sacramento. Over two point one million dollars were missing from that vault. Not including the one hundred and fifty grand that was missing from the cash tellers' registers. Once again, these guys weren't in this bank no longer than two minutes, and still were able to come out before the entire police force, that's only five minutes away, could block off the area. Now from my understanding. Detective Pakori and the Sacramento police department were actually arriving when these guys were leaving with tons of bags out of this building. This time we have one driver, two cars, and five gunmen who actually traded shots with Detective Pakori. The same detective who actually gunned one of these robbers down on the scene allowing the rest to make a sweet get away with half of the county's savings because of a personal vendetta." Shannon closed her folder and crossed her legs with a look of confidence. "Now I'm not the best at everything I do, because I suck at washing dishes, and doing laundry, but a blind homeless kid could clearly see that there is something wrong with this picture sir. Why did you kill the suspect instead of blocking off the area to take these guys down?"

Exhaling lightly. Detective Pakori sat back in his chair. "I did exactly what I was supposed to do, Detective. This was a critical situation, and unfortunately, I had a group of armed and dangerous hooligans prepared to kill officers and citizens of my city. It was either take one down or let them all go scot-free. I was trying to prevent the greater harm and blocking off the streets from six heavily armed men could have led to half of my force dying. You said it yourself, Shannon. These guys traded shots with over fifteen of my officers. Not fearing the outcome of anyone's safety being in jeopardy. I didn't see you out there protecting and serving your community in the mix of two undercovers dying, and four of my men being wounded. Matter of fact. I think you were out investigating miscellaneous traffic tickets while I was busting my ass to take these fuckers down. You're my best shooter at this department, but that day you were nowhere to be found. I guess that answers your question on how we couldn't tackle this situation. Shit doesn't smell good Shannon. It stinks for a reason, and unfortunately, we can't win them all, but never insult my status of being a good detective for this force, because I wouldn't do it to you. It was a bad day, and we all have them," Pakori said before placing his attention back on his laptop. "You're dismissed, now follow up the leads on your murder cases and leave this file to me.

Shannon smirked before standing to her feet. Heading for the door. She turned and looked at him with a stern expression. "Justice will be served, sir. F.B.I Agent Patrick Kegg will be serving you for the investigation of that man's death. He was shot in the leg first and after that, his back was blown out. That was an execution, and I'm afraid that cops don't kill. We protect. Good day sir." She smiled before walking out and closing the office door behind her.

***

Jabari's Crib
11:32 A.M.

Chris Green

Jumping out of the shower feeling extra refreshed. Jabari looked at himself in the mirror and rubbed a hand through his waves. After making sure his hygiene was on point. He exited the bathroom and tossed on a pair of Blue Burberry bleached jeans. His plain jane T-shirt was hand-stitched by Ferragamo, and a Burberry blue jean vest rested neatly on top of that giving him a nice, and smooth preppy swag for the day. Reaching under his bed. He pulled out a pair of all-white Ferragamo loafers. There was no need for any socks, especially with the soft Italian fabric that laid neatly on the inside of his fifteen-hundred-dollar slippers. Brandon's sixteenth birthday was coming soon and all he could think about was making sure his young champ received everything he deserved. It was hard being nineteen and providing for a kid who wasn't his, but that was the reason he was willing to lay his life down to get that bread by any means necessary. It was a process, but so was scheming righteous citizens out of their money. The government gave away benefits to certain individuals that needed it when they chose to and took tax dollars from the ones who worked hard daily to provide for their loved ones. Those same dollars were sliding right back into the pockets of the high class, at no cost because money ruled the nation, and you weren't talking about shit if you weren't toting any. People were blinded by the small handouts, and instead of them waking up to become their own bosses, they would rather waddle around in the establishments of the nearest McDonalds, or Kentucky Fried Chicken in order to feed their families check to check. It was a process of building a legacy for your own, but in order for it to work. A motherfucker had to be willing to go, and fight for what was theirs.

Counting out a cool five grand. He stashed it inside of his pants pockets and placed a blue Mitchell and Ness Carolina Panthers snapback on his head. Picking up his black Hublot fusion watch.

He applied it to his wrist and left out of his bedroom to head downstairs with the crew.

Blow, and Brandon sat on the couch indulging in a game of Mortal Kombat on the PlayStation 4. The living room was filled with weed smoke, and judging from the way Teddy was breaking down blunts at the dining table. They ass had no intentions on slowing down to let that bitch air out. "Has anyone of y'all special ed kids seen Leo?" Jabari asked, looking at the time on his watch.

"Nigga, we don't know. He's probably somewhere trying to figure out how to fuck his laptop." Blow laughed.

Just as he made that dumb ass comment. Leo came through the front door with his laptop in hand. The entire room stopped their movements and placed their attention directly on him. "What the fuck y'all looking at me like that for?" he asked while tapping a few buttons on his keyboard.

Everyone couldn't help but bust out laughing knowing the statement that was just made seconds before he came in. "I told you." Blow crashed against the floor holding his stomach. "This man is having an affair with his computer."

"Y'all niggas get off my boy. Don't hate 'cause he knows how to finesse a computer out of its panties, and y'all can't even find the internet explorer." Jabari chuckled before embracing his friend.

"Man, what the hell are y'all niggas in here talking about me for?" Leo asked. "And Blow, I know you ain't saying shit. You used my shit the other day, and I found some shit on there that can dub yo ass out the crew. I don't be on chicks with dicks, sir. I'm straight Pornhub." He laughed with his middle finger in the air.

"Ayo stop playing, bruh. I ain't never been with that gay shit. Now, we ain't gonna even play like that." Blow's face balled up after that everyone began to laugh at his ass.

"I know that's right. Stop making jokes then." Jabari chuckled before picking up one of Teddy's rolled blunts. "Nah, for real though y'all. I know we're supposed to be kicking shit today or whatnot, but y'all need to remember that we got some serious shit coming up in the next few weeks. I just want y'all to be on point. This is a casino we are talking about. It's not the average shit that we use to taking down so I'm gonna be clear on this shit. No talking or running your mouth about the business. One slip up, and we can be spending the rest of our lives in the underground railroad, or worse, Dead."

"Well, I'm not related to Harriet Tubman, and I'm damn sho' not ready to kick the bucket so my shit is sealed like a brick, baby." Teddy smiled.

"That sounds very good, but we don't know what a nigga would do when it comes down to thirty million dollars getting snagged from a casino. That shit will bring the army out, and I promise they gonna find some answers one way or another. I'll be setting up the process with Jabari, and then we will all meet a week before the movement to ensure that there are no slips. Besides that, y'all niggas suck it easy until then," Leo said before walking into the kitchen.

"That nigga gay for real." Blow nodded towards him as he walked away.

Before Jabari could reply. His phone began to vibrate lightly in his pocket. Digging inside to retrieve it. He answered, "Yeah, who this?"

"Hi. This is Doctor Philmore Anderson from the Mercy General Hospital. I'm looking for Jabari Salters."

Taking a second look at the number. He placed it back to his ear, moving a small distance away from the crew. "This is me, any specific reason you calling my phone?"

"Um, yes sir. I have a patient at the hospital who's in the intensive care unit. She's requested to see you, but I'm afraid that I can't give any information out over the phone. Are you available to stop by sir?"

That statement alone caused his heart to flutter, and Victoria flashed through his mind. "Yes. I'll be there in twenty minutes," he agreed before hanging up.

Stepping back over to the crew. He paused miscellaneous conversation. "Aye listen. Something just came up, so I gotta make a run. I'll meet y'all as soon as I'm done. Lock up my crib."

"Hell nah, bro. You said this was our day. All that political Black Panther shit needs to wait. You can miss a day or two of being in serious mode." Brandon paused the game, looking back at him.

"It's something different. I promise. I'll meet y'all after I'm done, but I gotta go," Jabari stated before rushing out of the front door.

Blow sat his controller down after the front door closed. "Well guess what? That nigga ain't about to kill our vibe for today. We fucking some bitches and getting blistered. I need you to handle something with me first though. You down to bust a move or what?" He looked over at Brandon with a stale face.

"What kind of move?"

"Business. Somebody has been doing a little too much talking, and you just heard what Jabari and Leo said. We can't allow any nigga's loose ass lips to sink this ship. It's something in it for you too," Blow whispered lightly so Leo couldn't eavesdrop.

Brandon pondered a second before accepting his invitation. "I'm down."

"Cool. Say, Teddy. Wassup lil nigga? You riding with us or what?"

"Hell yeah. Especially if some hoes are involved. I'm not trying to be sitting here catching viruses with ya boy Leo's freaky ass," he replied, grabbing all the rolled joints of marijuana.

Grabbing two of Jabari's handguns from under his couch, Blow passed Brandon one and placed the other one on his hip. "We'll be back later, grandma." He flicked a bird at Leo before they left out of the crib.

Chapter 2
Old Sacramento
The Slums

Pulling into the parking lot of the three-bedroom home Blow, Brandon, and Teddy climbed out of the car and headed for the front door. The nasty neighborhood in Old Sacramento was beyond crooked. Niggas on that side of town only played one way, and that was for keeps. Most of the gangstas growing up around their way were either Blood Gang or a fucking Mexican. It was treacherous if you didn't know what location you were pulling down into, so niggas made sure to be careful about how they stepped across the grass around the territory. Especially niggas from Hagginwood.

Stepping on the front porch. Blow took the lead, knocking on the door. A small shuffle of noise could be heard from the inside before the door came flying open. Rarri, the known drug dealer in the neighborhood, clutched on his Ak-47 with a menacing snarl as if everybody standing on his porch was about to die. Brandon slightly flinched from the reaction of the dumb nigga's demeanor, but he could tell from the way Blow remained calm that shit wasn't about to get out of control.

"Blow, why the hell you showing up three deep to my spot dawg? You know I be booting up during daylight, bro," Rarri said looking back, and forth between them all.

"Nigga, we need to talk. You sent that reckless ass message to my phone, so I came to see what the hell you crying about. Is you gonna let us in or not?" he replied, holding up a handful of blunts.

Wiping his nose with a backhand. He smiled and let the crew inside. Once they all crossed the threshold. He locked the door and took a seat back on the couch in front of his nose candy.

"You guys booting or what?" he asked, pushing the plate across the glass table.

21

Blow sat on the couch, and Brandon followed suit taking a seat beside him. "Nah, me and my lil niggas good. Like I said, I'm talking about that message. What the hell makes you think I cut you out of a deal bruh. You didn't have in on this bank Rarri?

"Are you crazy, nigga? I gave you all the straps Blow. You didn't even have enough respect to bring me my fucking burners back. I told you from the jump that I wanted a hundred racks, and if you couldn't handle that end of the bargain you shouldn't have taken my shit," Rarri spat leaning back on his couch.

Huffing lightly. Blow rotated his eyes over to Brandon and looked back at Rarri. "You right, but nigga, you can calm down with all that big dawg shit. We all grown here, and I can hear you without all that fake ass aggressive shit."

"Aye, I'm not trying to interrupt big dawg, but do you mind if I use your bathroom? I gotta shit bad." Brandon balled up his face as if his stomach was extra fucked up.

Rarri fired up one of Blow's blunt and gave him a nasty expression. "Straight to the back, and don't blow my shit up without using the air freshener," he said before placing his attention back to the conversation at hand.

Teddy was still standing to the side when Brandon stood up and walked behind the couch. Rarri never noticed the gun that he pulled from his waist until the room grew quiet. By that time. It was too fucking late. Brandon pulled the trigger once sending a slug through the back of his cranium. "Boom!

His head crashed against the glass table shattering it to pieces. He wasted no time standing over him and firing six more shots into his skull.

Boc! Boc! Boc! Boc! Boc! Boc!

Blow was sure to jump up from his spot to ensure that none of Rarri's blood spilled on him. "God damn nigga. I said shoot em one time, not seven. What the fuck?"

Brandon held the gun as if he did something wrong. "I didn't know if he would die from one bullet, nigga. He got this big ass AK sitting next to him. I had to make sure." He shrugged his shoulders.

"Boy, you just really snapped. I would have thought that nigga kidnapped your daughter or some shit. Y'all niggas on some real Taken shit around this bitch," Teddy interrupted flicking his weed roach in the ashtray. "Can I have this pretty ass gun?" He smiled picking up Rarri's assault rifle.

Blow wasted no time pulling out two sets of rubber gloves passing them both a pair. "Y'all can have whatever y'all want out this bitch. First, let's rip this bitch up and get the hell out of here. This nigga is a brick man, so we need to move fast now!"

Teddy shrugged. "You ain't gotta tell me twice. Baby boy already starting to smell like a can of sardines," he snickered before rushing upstairs.

Blow looked over to Brandon who slid his gloves on with ease. Checking his watch, he smiled. "We got two minutes young one. I'll meet y'all out front."

"You know it," Brandon replied, heading for the kitchen.

***

Mercy General Hospital
Sacramento, California

Stepping off the elevator, Jabari moved quickly towards the front desk and tapped the counter lightly to get the nurse's attention. "Excuse me, ma'am. I'm looking for a Doctor Philmore Anderson."

Before she could answer, a white man with a grey beard tapped his shoulder. "You must be Jabari."

Turning around, Jabari looked at the older man with an inquisitive eye. His hair was slightly disheveling at the top. A gold Rolex submariner watch was dangling on his right wrist, and a clipboard filled with tons of papers was resting underneath his armpit. You could tell from his round glasses and stern look that he had to be the head Doctor around the hospital for sure. "Yes sir. Your call sounded urgent. What's the emergency?" Jabari questioned, folding his arms.

"Follow me, sir." He started to walk down the hallway behind him.

Jabari trailed quickly behind him praying that nothing was wrong with Victoria, Cynthia, or his mother. Hospitals only meant one thing. Pregnancies, or death. It would be hard to hear any bad news after so much shit was already occurring at the moment, but it was no such thing as turning around or denying the doctor's request.

After bending a few corners. They ended up inside the Intensive Care Unit. The doctor used a small I'D badge to enter the small, sectioned area. A few rooms aligned the walls, and he continued to walk until he reached medical door number eight. Turning around to look at Jabari. He shook his hand firmly. "This is where I depart. Please let me know if you need anything, or if there's any problem. I'll be right over there at the first office on the right. "He explained before walking off.

Jabari nodded before taking a deep breath. Placing his hand on the door handle. He pushed it open lightly and walked inside. The sounds from the breathing machines, and were beeping at a low pace, while a small monitor scanner was showing the pulse of a heartbeat moving gently as a brisk of wind. The woman who laid on the bed was facing the opposite way from Jabari forcing him to walk on the other side of her. Once he noticed that it was Steven's mother, Ms. Morgan, her eyes opened slowly locking in on him.

"HI, Jabari. It's good to see you, darling," she whispered as if her voice was hurting painfully.

"Oh my God! Ms. Morgan. What happened to you?" He climbed down on one knee inching towards the bed.

"Well, as they say, us old people eventually get sick, and then we do the worst after we expect the best. Kick the bucket. I'm so glad you could make it." She coughed lightly into her hand.

Jabari nearly shed a tear from the condition Ms. Morgan was in currently. Her eyelids were slightly swollen. The normal weight that she used to have was now down to at least seventy-five pounds, and her full head of hair was now thinning out. All he could do was gently grab ahold of her hand. "Ms. Morgan, what happened to you? I haven't seen you or Steven in almost two years. It's like both of y'all disappeared."

"Steven is and will always be okay. I can't say the same thing for myself. Unfortunately, I caught a bad case of lung cancer and I'm dying, Jabari. It's nothing that I can really be upset with my God about. I've tried therapy classes. I've had some of the best doctors prescribe me all the so-called good medicine, but still in all, my body continues to reject all of it. It's been exactly two weeks since this demon has gotten a hold of me and it's finally winning, Jabari. Truly, it's nothing that I want you to be sad about darling. It's the reason I asked to see you," she explained, coughing into her hand again.

Rubbing her fingers lightly, he forced a smile on his face. "I'm glad that you still thought of me at such a critical moment. Is there anything that I can do for you? Whatever you need, you got it. Anything Mama Morgan."

Watching her chest heave slowly, she paused a second before speaking. "All I want you to do is listen because I have a lot to tell you, son. Only if you have the time to give little old Ms. Morgan a minute."

Her words were sincere, and he could definitely tell that it was something important from the way she was speaking. "Yes ma'am."

"Ever since you and Steven became friends as little children, I knew that you would be special. I saw a significant light inside of you that I see in no other. From the way you would help Brandon and Steven focus, while being present even with the miscellaneous things you've created around Hagginwood. You never let your brightness dim out because of the negativity around you. I can't say the same for Steven 'cause I feel that he was beginning to lose focus. Not from you, but from the individuals who were around you all. Everyone can't be as smart as you, Jabari. For you to be so young, I would've thought that your brother, Kentavious, and that rascal Blow could have actually gained some knowledge from you."

Hearing the name Kentavious caused his heart to flutter because that same name came from his mother, Crystal's, mouth fluently. The scary part was the word brother that came from between Ms. Morgan's lips. "Mama Morgan, I don't have a brother named Kentavious."

Even the sickness couldn't stop the funny expression she gave Jabari when he made the awkward statement. "Son, I'm sixty-one years old. I'm quite sure of what I'm speaking about. How could you hang with these older boys night and day, and look me in the eyes to say that he isn't your brother? I'm not that old."

Jabari thought hard before speaking, but he was quite sure who she was talking about "Are you referring to Keyno?"

"Keylo, Keybo, I'm not positive about all that mess. Crystal Salters named her son Kentavious Williams, and that I am sure of. Second, you have Jabari Salters and Brandon Salters. It was three boys that came out of that woman, and I was around to see all of y'all come home with her from this same hospital I'm resting in now."

Jabari's ears couldn't believe what he was taking in at that moment. "Are you telling me that Keyno was my older brother? His face seemed more hurt than surprised.

"That's like asking me if Sacramento is a city inside of California Jabari. Yes, he is your brother. Ronald never told you this?" she asked with a raised eyebrow.

All he could do was shake his head, but really his emotions were clawing at his heart to release a barrel of tears at that moment.

"Oh goodness. Well, I guess I got a little more to explain than I thought. I'm not too good with beating around the bushes as they say, but your daddy, Ronald, took that boy away from your mama when he was no more than seven or eight. He hated that child because he wasn't his. That was Kenneth's boy. Your dad was in love with Crystal, but he couldn't accept the fact that she had a child with one of his so-called gangster buddies. She respected Kenneth, but their relationship days were over around the time she connected with Ronald. He was so jealous. More jealous than a man could ever be about a woman who was raising another man's child. I watched these same guys who claimed the streets of Sacramento fall out as if they were never best friends. Then one day, Kenneth was found dead. It was a shocker for everybody because we knew that it would be a price to pay for whoever pulled that vicious act. Jubbie and Ronald didn't play when it came down to Kenneth because they only trusted each other."

The name Jubbie danced through Jabari's mind, and a small flashback of the night he robbed his first gambling house ignited like a wildfire. Instead of stopping her, he kept his lips sealed and continued to listen.

"What we thought was a murder began to look like a set-up because months and months went by with no sight or word from

Jubbie or Ronald. You rarely saw Crystal leave outside of that house, and when she did, he was clinging on to her tighter than a handcuff. She was starting to change. Her appearance, her beauty. The way she moved around Hagginwood with joy. I'd seen that look too many times to know what it was, and I knew that she would never be the same." Ms. Morgan pointed her shaking finger lightly.

"What do you mean she wouldn't be the same, Mama Morgan?" Jabari asked with a large ball of rage in his heart for the bitch nigga Ronald. He still was standing firm on not letting that shit show.

"That man was making Crystal smoke that poison. The same damn poison Jubbie was selling to everybody and their mama in the neighborhood. He had her mind so gone that he was able to basically send Kentavious right on out to the nearest foster care center. The sight of the boy being around was eating at his flesh, and that's when I knew he had something to do with Kenneth being murdered. This went on until you and Brandon were born. By the time you were four, Crystal was a full course addict and your father was being arrested and heading down to Pelican Bay for a fifteen-year sentence. He and Jubbie felt they owned the world until the neighborhood started to talk. It was always better to be loved than feared, but it was the opposite way around for those two. I watched y'all boys live with friends of the family. Group home to group home. All because of your daddy not wanting to raise Kentavious. He polluted your mom's mind to think that the boy didn't even exist."

"How come you never told me any of this before Ms. Morgan? I've sat back my entire life thinking that my mom's addiction was by her own choice."

"Because sweetheart, I'm not superwoman. I can only say so much when you have an entire family around who won't say anything at all. Just because I'm a little old white woman who lived in Hagginwood for forty years doesn't mean that I can place my nose into everything I smell that's funny, baby. In a certain way, I felt that it could harm you, but also protect you. Your peace and mind were so great that my stories could have detoured you from doing other things. You're not a robber and killer like your dad and older brother. You're smarter," she said, grabbing a hold of his hand tighter.

Holding his head down, he took in the new info and decided to make his own journey from that day forth. Regardless of how Ms. Morgan felt, those situations she laid upon him just opened a new door for the way he was going to move around the streets of Sacramento. Not only was his new hatred for Ronald risen to the max, but the dream that he had of Keyno was a true message that his mother deserved to know. "Thank you, Ms. Morgan. I truly needed that."

"Jabari that's not it." She looked at him with all seriousness lacing her sick pupils.

Turning his head to the side. He flashed her a curious expression. "What do you mean?"

"That demon Blow who sticks around you. He's no-good, Jabari. He killed Ronald. He shot him that night in the parking lot of the store, and he's trying to hide it from you. We all know that people can die in Hagginwood for speaking too much, but I'm close to leaving this place soon," she admitted and placed a small piece of paper in his hand. "You'll always be protected and watched over. I'm begging you Jabari. Make him pay. He's the devil reincarnated, and if you don't take care of him. He's gonna knock you down until you can't stand again. I truly love you soon, and I'll never forget how you took care of my son."

Her last remark caused a small tear to drop from his eye. The slimeball Blow was the first suspect in his mind, especially when he offered to pay for the entire funeral. Ever since that day, Blow made it his business to stay close to the team, and he was surely playing his part better than a Beethoven's special. Leaning down to kiss Ms. Morgan on her cheek, he looked her directly in the eyes. "I love you, Mama Morgan. Thank you so much. Is there anything I can do for you while you're here?"

"No son. You can hold that information in your hand close to your heart and take my advice on what I said. You're like a son to me. I have faith that you could be a king in this city if you want." She forced a big smile for him.

That remark alone felt as if it gave him the power of an immortal. He was gonna be sure to make that become truer than anyone could ever expect. "Yes ma'am. I promise I will," he replied before walking out of her medical room.

Unfolding the paper that she gave him, he stared at the number and dialed it into his phone. Jabari waited until he exited the hospital to press dial. The call was answered after the second ring, and he never got a chance to speak once the voice spoke through the line. "Please don't speak. Just listen. A message will appear on your phone in the next few seconds. Read it," the man informed him before hanging up.

Glancing at his phone with a weird look, he jumped in his new Dodge Durango SRT and started the engine. The sound of a message appearing on his line forced him to open it quickly. Staring at the picture on his screen, his eyes grew wide in shock. Placing his car in drive, he exited the hospital's parking lot and headed back for his home. Stopping at the first red light, Jabari's eyes happened to rotate to his rearview mirror. The same black Charger that followed him down to Mercy General was back on his bumper, and it was now clear who was sitting behind the passenger seat. If they thought shit was sweet, they were definitely madly mistaking because Jabari was surely on point. As the light turned green, he made the first right, and just as he figured, the Charger made the turn with him. They were sure to stay at least thirty feet away from his vehicle like it was going unnoticed, but the young mastermind was smarter than the average robber. After laying so many niggas down, you became accustomed to knowing when a person was trailing your every step. Being sure to keep a close eye on the car, he quickly dialed Brandon's number. It didn't take but a few rings for his little brother to pick up.

"Yo Bari."

"Where are y'all?" he asked, accelerating on his gas pedal lightly. Sure enough, the car behind him began to pick up a little speed.

"We're over at Blow's condo. We got a few people over kicking shit. Where are you, man? Come have some fun, bro. You be trying to work too damn much," he replied in a slurred tone as if he was drunk.

"Why the fuck do you sound like that?

"I'm just a little buzzed bro. It's nothing. Are you coming over?"

"Yeah, but I got a little something going on right now. I need you to be on point. I'm going to check in a room at a hotel downtown. If you get a message from me after this call, bring the crew and come get me asap," he explained while making his way to the destination.

"Are you sure you good, Bari?" Brandon asked with more worry in his tone.

"I'm good. Just remember what I said." He hung up the line and sat his black Glock 23 pistol on his lap. He didn't know what his secret admirer had planned, but it was only going one way, and that was the Kingz way. He was willing to bet his life on that shit.

***

The Hilton Hotel
Twenty Minutes Later

Walking through the lobby of the hotel, Jabari took a few minutes to finesse his way up to the counter and have a fruitless conversation with the clerk. Grabbing a desk card from the small clear holder, he cut his eyes to see if the secret follower had enough guts to trail him inside of the luxury building. Just as he expected. The chase was on, and this brave stalker was truly determined. Keeping his cool, he stuck with the plan and made his way towards the elevator. It didn't take long for him to get on and press the button for the tenth floor. If the games were going to be played, it was definitely gonna be by his rules.

***

Shannon moved quickly around the corner towards the elevators to catch sight of Jabari before she lost sight of him. Just as she hit the corner she caught sight of the doors closing. Being patient to see which floor the light stopped on, Shannon inhaled deeply. Once It reached ten, she flew quickly up the flight of stairs that sat directly next to elevator doors. Her Louis Vuitton sneakers and loose-fitting sweats made it easy for her to leap the stairs as if she was on *Survival of the Fittest*. Pushing it up to the tenth floor, she caught a breather before sliding through the side door. A glimpse of him could be seen entering room 1043. Pressing against the corner of the wall, she peeked around the edge and took her chances moving forward. Sliding down to room 1043, Shannon could see that the door was slightly cracked. A voice could be heard speaking in a moderate tone inside. The conversation she heard began to grow, and it was obvious that he was singing to himself. When the thought crossed her mind to ease it open, the barrel of a gun was pressed deeply into her back.

"If you buck, I'll kill you," Jabari whispered, removing the gun from her waistband.

His voice flushed down her spine causing the hairs on Shannon's neck to stand up. He wasn't forceful, but the light push he gave her stated that he meant business. "Walk in."

His feet moved behind her until they ended up inside the hotel suite. Jabari held her from behind as if they were a happy couple once they stepped in front of the butler who was dusting the kitchen counter.

"Uhh, it seems that I found my wife. You can cancel the cleaning session, sir." He smiled with the gun pressed into her back.

Shannon flashed a fake smile being sure not to anger a full-hearted criminal mastermind. There was no telling how far he would take the stunt, and she wasn't trying to be a casualty on an unapproved follow investigation.

The Caucasian male nodded. "Thanks for the hundred-dollar tip, sir." He swiftly moved past them and left out of the room and the door closed gently behind him.

"I don't know who you think-"

"Shut the fuck up please. I'll be the one speaking during this process."

"Listen, buddy. I'd like to let you know that I'm a cop," she blurted out. There was no solid answer as to if she would leave that hotel alive, but she damn sure wasn't about to lay down without trying everything in her natural cop instincts.

"I kinda figured that when I saw the gun and shiny pair of circle thingies on your hip. I didn't ask you that, neither did I tell you to speak, Detective Shannon," Jabari said in a calm manner.

The pressure on her chest tightened when her name rolled off of his tongue like Crisco grease. Not only did he say it with ease, but his tone alone also gave her the feeling that Jabari knew she was coming. "How did you know my name?"

"I said I'm the one in charge. I'll be clear when I say this Detective. I know everything about you. The history in the law field. The immaculate grade point average from Yale. The crooked dealings with the Sacramento Police Department. I can promise you this, if you buck, I'm gonna spread your body out across the Pacific until the sea turtles nibble your ashes away. Place your hands behind your back and follow my orders."

Swallowing her spit in fear, the comment caused Shannon's stomach to bubble. It was always her mission to be cautious when dealing with a criminal, but his slight breakdown of her bio was enough to convince her that he wasn't playing the same games as the past free cases she gently swept away.

Doing as she was told, she placed her hands backwards expecting him to put the cuffs on her.

"Stand in military position."

"Excuse me?

"Captain on deck. Stand at attention," he barked a little louder.

Standing straight as an arrow, she locked her legs pushing her plump, and round bottom out like a sore thumb. Her eyes were staring at the walls like a dart target. She wanted to see his face. It took everything in her power to not turn around and try his weak ass gangsta. That good ass gut feeling continued to warn her otherwise. Just when things got silent for a second too long, he made his next command.

"Now pull down your clothes and hike that ass up on the bed. Slow," he emphasized his words so Shannon could know that it was official.

"So, you're a rapist?" Her teeth gritted in anger. Jabari was moving behind her like a phantom waiting to cause his victim a massive heart attack.

"Bend ova and find out!" he snapped.

Jumping from his voice, she envisioned the gun blowing out her lower back. Mr. Criminal was being a dickhead, and now he was ordering shit that wasn't on the menu. Using her hands, she roughly pulled her sweats and panties down to her ankles and arched up nicely on the bed.

"Do you want an order of fries with that because you're gonna need them after you get stuffed under the biggest maximum-security prison I can find if you touch me bastard," Shannon hissed with her face down on the mattress. Jabari gazed at her perfectly shaven kitten. Her pretty pink kitty lips purred in anger with every breath she took. Her thighs were nice and chunky. It could force a racist to believe that she had a little bit of black in her bones.

Tossing the handcuffs in front of her, he cleared his throat. "Put them on both wrists, and don't move out of that position."

Huffing, she grabbed the cuffs and clinked them lightly on her wrist leaving just enough to slide her slim hands out of the thick metal links and being sure to play her role. She picked his brain to see where his evil thoughts were about to lead off. "Do you feel safer, Mr. Animal?"

"Yeah, I do. So now that I'm more comfortable, we're gonna play a game. It's called guess what I am. Now, the rules are simple. I'll give you a few of my traits, and you'll have three tries to tell me what I am. If you lose, I'll kill you and walk out the front door. If you guess right, drop it all, and leave. That shouldn't be hard for a woman of your caliber. Right?" he asked, trailing a finger down her inner back.

"Just get it over with creep!"

"After my game." Jabari fiercely slapped her ass forcefully with his free hand.

"Aghhh! You motherfucker. I'll play the damn game. I'll take the game." She wobbled her head in a complying manner.

"Keep your fucking head down or its lights out!" He was now standing behind her arched behind, heaving lightly as Hannibal sliced open one of his victims.

Huffing with anger. She calmed herself as he trailed the barrel down her deep arch. She fidgeted from the cold steel knowing that it could erupt at any minute.

"My game is simple. You'll listen to my characteristics and tell me what I am since you know me so well, Ms. Kegg."

He could tell by the way that her body was slightly shivering that she was nervous. It was all a part of his plan to rise and conquer. Mind games were a critical part of life. And if you didn't know the difference between the truth and some game, yo ass was bound to drown.

"Now, I'm a taker most of the time. I search, and study most of the time using my great charm to fitness, and gain entrance," He spoke while massaging the gun right above the crack of her ass. Her eyes closed feeling a slight bubble rise in her stomach.

"Once I gain entrance, I drain you. I get all that you have to offer until there is nothing for me to clean out of your system. I move swiftly but take my time as I pace around to handle the business. I'm a guaranteed satisfaction to handle the objective. I'm a beast at what I do, and it's even caused some to never shake back from all that I had to offer." He was now trailing a finger down her crack until he reached her kitty lips. Shannon closed her eyes while biting on her lips in a dark state of mind. The sound of his voice was forcing her legs to quiver, and the feeling between her legs was about to crack like an overheated water pipe. Tracing her pussy with two fingers.

He asked his next question in a strong voice, "Tell me what I am, Shannon." Now his fingers were slowly crawling inside of her milky split.

Releasing a light moan. She uttered the first word that came to mind. "You're a fucking womanizerrr!"

"Good," he replied, digging his finger deeper and forcing her to jump. "Ssss… you bastard. What are you doing to me?"

"I'm giving you the breakdown of the man you're chasing. You searched until you found me. Now, what's next?"

"I don't know who I'm looking for. I'm just doing my fucking job, cocksucker!" she whimpered. "Release me and I'll spare you on that million-year plea, you scumbag."

"Look back at me," Jabari ordered.

Shannon was shocked by his request, but she didn't want to show him her excitement to get a close look at the man they call Jabari Salters. As her head adjusted to look behind her, he was standing with a serious mug on his face. His eyes were matching hers, and he didn't flinch when she roamed her eyes down to his manhood hanging from the zipper. Before she could do any rejections, he grabbed her hip and slipped directly into her warm pussy.

"Jesusss!" She raised her back like a kitten from his length.

Leaning down to give her ass a flick from his warm tongue. She fidgeted. Rising, he held the gun in his other hand while pumping forcefully inside her kitty. Her womanhood was dripping in euphoria, and the sad thing that had her stuck was the way he laid down his D game. He was a bad boy with the traits of a freak.

The feeling of his dick dumping down into her belly caused Shannon to whine in pleasure. "Why are you doing thisss?" She panted, pressing her face against the pillow. His shit was ripping the lining out her tight coochie, and she was trembling with every stroke he delivered. Her ass clapped gently against his pelvis, and it was with no effort. The mind game was now on Shannon, and she was playing it to the T. Throwing that ass back, she made sure to stare Jabari directly in the eyes. His athletic body flexed his amazing pecs every time he slid inside.

"I'm gonna show you that I'm not comfortable with being followed. Do you understand me, Detective Kegg?"

"I understand." She cringed, feeling a massive orgasm spilling down her leg. Shannon's eyes felt heavy as if glue was trying to hold them closed. The way Jabari pounded inside of her, began to form a sticky rim of cum around her sweet spot. Reaching over her, he grabbed her wrist clinching the cuffs tighter. By the time she realized what he was doing, it too was late.

"That should hold you a little longer." He laughed smoothly into her ear.

Shaking the nasty orgasm from her thoughts. She snapped back into reality. "Youuu son of a bitchhh! Let me out of these cuffs! I did what you asked."

Rolling Shannon over to her back, she squirmed recklessly before looking up into his eyes.

Watching him buckle up his jeans, he grabbed a soft pillow placing it three feet away from her head. Jabari raised the keys for the cuffs and sat them directly on top. "There you go beautiful. The next time that you feel you can try to hunt me down, don't. Your guess about me is probably right, but there is only one thing that makes your determined little chase worthless." He leaned down towards her; she was breathing heavily through her nostrils.

"I love my job just as much as you love yours. Banks are like a candy store. You slide in and run out until you can't anymore. Unfortunately, I'm too full of sugar, and my race is far from over." Jabari slid her pistol back on his hip. "Have a good day, Kegg." He smiled before turning to leave.

"I'll bury you for this shit. I've seen your face, idiot. We know it's you committing these robberies Jabari. There's no way to make it away from us. We are this city," she stated as if he would surely be in the Sacramento County Jail by morning.

Shrugging his shoulders, he gave her a nonchalant expression. "I can die any day, Detective. You might wanna hurry," his voice trailed off as he exited the room leaving Shannon to break free on her own.

Rolling towards the pillow, Shannon took a deep breath and brushed against it to bring the key closer. The hard rock forced it to go over the edge, and once the silver keys slapped against the floor. She knew that it was about to be a long night.

Chris Green

Chapter 3
Blow's Condo
2 hours later

The loud music that was playing could be heard outside of Blow's studio apartment door. The beat from the bass of his speakers quacked as if the niggas was throwing freak'nik for a bunch of Atlanta pro's, and Zaxby's cashiers. Jabari knocked firmly on the door ensuring that he wasn't about to stand out in the hallway all day. A few seconds later. The chains could be heard releasing, and the door opened slowly. Sip peeped out and looked at Jabari.

"Damn nigga. I thought you were the police beating on that bitch like that bro. No rap cap. That was way too hard my guy," his squeaky voice rattled Jabari's ears forcing him to move straight past him, with a small bump to the shoulder.

Blow sat at the kitchen's table with a girl's face inside of his lap. The disturbing part was Brandon sitting next to him with his face occupied in a small pile of cocaine. Jabari's face wrinkled, his temper instantly shot through the roof, he paced slowly over to them. Teddy was knocked out in a chair with his head in the air, and they never expected to be caught red-handed until Brandon raised his head from the table.

"What the fuck is that?" Jabari spat, startling them both.

"It's molly, and why the fuck you ain't call before just popping up to my crib? I thought you were the pizza man." Blow pushed the chick's head from his lap.

"Brandon, you don't even know what the hell this is, and you tryna follow this nigga shoving it up your damn nose! What's wrong with you?" he fumed with a vein protruding out of his neck.

"It was just one time, Jabari. Relax man, damn." Brandon stood to his feet with a smile.

Jabari slapped him across the face trying to knock some sense into his ass. Blow jumped to his feet, into Jabari's face as if he was about to save him.

"Nigga, you ain't have to hit lil bro like that."

The fist that collided with his jaw forced him to the floor hard. Teddy jumped up from his sleep, witnessing his buddies scrapping like two dogs on the street. Brandon's young ass was trying his best to split them apart while they struggled to rip each other's head off. Knowing that shit was about to get out of hand, he exhaled before running over to break them apart. "Can you niggas please stop this shit because I can't explain how a murder happened between y'all niggas? Chill out!" he yelled, forcing the action to cease.

"Fuck that nigga! I'm seconds away from killing you fool. You got my little one snorting molly like he's grown around this bitch! He's fifteen. Ever since he's been around you, he's gotten this fake ass demeanor, and that shit is gonna end tonight." Jabari pointed a stiff finger towards him.

Blow caught his breath and rubbed his eye that was now swelling by the second. His rage was fuming at the moment, and he didn't think before speaking the shit that was on his mind, "It's yo fault ya lil brother don't like you, nigga. You don't let him do shit. You treat him like a fucking lame, and he's just too scared to admit that he fucks with me harder than you. Ask him, nigga! Look at Brandon and ask if he even respects his own big brother!" Blow barked.

"Hey, listen the fuck up. That doesn't have shit to do with you, Blow. These niggas are brothers. We gotta let them handle personal shit on their own." Teddy stressed. "Now I don't know about you two, but we got something in line to set us good for life. I wanna see that happen. Not fall out with my team before I get a chance to live my shit."

"Yo whatever, nigga. He's my little brother, and I don't know about you, but he's all that I got left. I tell you niggas to watch a fifteen-year-old for a few hours, you clowns turn him into more of a problem than he already is." Jabari's veins were bulging out of his head. The way his fist was clenched, you could tell that he was trying hard not to explode.

"I understand all that." Teddy followed up his sentence. "Did I tell you that I'll go forty years without wiping my ass for thirty million dollars? We have an opportunity here."

"And I'm trying to see that shit happen!" Blow yelled.

"Act like it and try harder nigga. That's how you earn my respect idiot. Show my little one something better than what we do. Its already bad enough he's around, I refuse to let him turn into something that he wasn't ever meant to be."

Brandon stood to the side hoping that shit didn't get critical. Digging in his Zara jeans, he pulled out his car keys. "I'll just go home, bro. You embarrassing me, yo." He moved towards the front door.

Jabari moved swiftly behind him, grabbing his arm. "Hey champ, you've been drinking. I'll have Teddy drop it off later on and you'll ride home with me."

"Whatever," he mumbled, walking out of the front door. Jabari was sure to glance back at Blow before slamming the door.

Teddy looked over to him and before he could utter a word, Blow grabbed one of his barstools, crashing it across the wall. Pieces of shrubby wood scattered wildly, and his nose was flaring like an angry bull on rodeo night. Instead of offering his opinion, Teddy decided to let him vent and stepped out on the patio porch. It didn't take long before Blow stepped outside behind him with a glass of Belvedere in his hand. Stepping up to the rail, he inhaled the cool wind and took a deep breath.

"If this fool allows his punk ass emotions to get in the way of this money, he was never down with us from the jump. I'll kill'em," he snarled, glancing over at Teddy. He was picking with his fingernails as if the conversation didn't sound like a fire truck speeding down a project neighborhood street.

"Man, Jabari is gonna be Jabari, but that don't mean we should let that change us. He's gonna be ready when it's time. We just have to let him be for now. You know just like I know that he ain't about to pass up no damn twenty million. Remember that taking is the way this nigga been eating since we were sixteen. Be easy and let it be until we can see how this shit unfolds," Teddy explained with a hand on his shoulder. The sound of the traffic below them.

Blow smiled wickedly and held up his glass. The city was shining beautifully. His exquisite condo apartment was one of the best on the block, and the check he always dreamed of having was finally coming true, but Jabari was starting to be that dull ass cloud, lingering around and hating like a muthafucka. It was now a choice. They were either gonna make money together or become each other's reapers. And money, the root of evil, would be the deciding factor.

Chapter 5
The next morning at 7:21. A.M.

The creaky sound of the hotel door opening caused Shannon's eyes to flutter open with nervousness. Jabari bounded and fucked her as if she was in the nearest freak spot on the avenue of 96 and Clarkston. She was still lying face-first on the cotton sheets like the maid service was coming to help with the cleanup, and all Shannon could vision was Jabari sending some off-brand dickhead who wanted to earn a reputation of finishing the job.

When her visitor stepped from behind the blind wall. Shannon's chest heaved before relaxing. She was the last face expected to be seen, especially after the fucked-up position Shannon happened to run across last night.

"Oh my God Shannon, Are you okay? Sarah stumbled over to her side, patting her to see if there were any wounds or signs of blood.

"The key! Get the key, Sarah." She shuffled and pointed her nose towards the small cuff key laying at the head of the mattress.

Quickly snatching it up, she released her from the restraints. "What happened? You leave and claim that you'll be back for dinner. Now, I get a call saying to get down to the hotel or I'll never see you again."

Shannon grabbed her wrist, rubbing them lightly, thinking about the way Jabari violated her. The situation was past the duties of their cornball police department. It was a critical case that was meant for a personal one on one She was gonna be sure that he received the worst death possible for the violation of her coochie, not to mention that she still couldn't get the necessary information she needed for a green light on investigating Jabari in the first place.

"Well, thanks for following the killer's instructions. You could've gotten yourself killed, Sarah. Why didn't you call dad?" Shannon stumbled around the room looking for any trace of Jabari that could've possibly been left behind.

"Because I didn't know if there would be someone here ready to hurt you if I made the wrong call Shannon. I was talking to my friend Jabari last night and right after that, a strange call came in alerting me that you were in trouble. Who put you in cuffs and what are you doing here in this first place?"

Hearing Jabari's name, Shannon rushed over to her, placing a hand over Sarah's mouth. She whispered, "How in the hell do you know his name? Are you involved with these guys?"

Removing Shannon's hand, Sarah huffed. "What are you talking about? Jabari is just a friend of mine. What does he have to do with you?"

"I'm doing an investigation on Jabari Salters for the recent bank robberies that's occurred in Sacramento."

Sarah's face dropped like a ton of bricks from a collapsing building once her sister spilled Jabari's last name. Instead of playing Shannon to the left as if she didn't know, Sarah took off running for the door as if she was the number one suspect.

Tackling her to the floor, Shannon held her down while she struggled to get free.

"Get off me! I don't know anything, Shannon. I swear." Her lies were sliding out faster than a Dodge Hellcat in the rain.

"I never asked you about Jabari, Sarah. Now tell me what the fuck is going on, and I mean now. This is a federal investigation dealing with five armed and dangerous men who're knocking down daddy's city. You know him, don't you?" Shannon questioned with a straight face.

Sarah's eyes began to water lightly. Her large sniffles and fluttering eyelids gave Shannon all the closure she needed for an answer. "Did you fuck him, Shannon? I can see it all over your face."

"What?

"Don't play stupid now Ms. goodie. I can see it all over your nasty face. You're bounded in a hotel. Facedown, ass up. Handcuffs? You tried to chase him, didn't you?" Sarah grilled her.

Shannon stumbled over her words before releasing her sister. "This has nothing to do with me, Sarah. You're telling me that you've been involved with a man who's suspected of robbing nine banks. Doesn't that seem serious to you? Doesn't it?" she yelled a little louder.

Sarah rolled her eyes, folded her arms, and smirked. "Suspected, means not positive. It sounds like you're on another mission to fuck my next boyfriend instead of doing your job. If you don't mind. I have somewhere to be. I don't wanna stop your precious investigation," Sarah said sarcastically before heading towards the door. "Oh, and before I forget. Try to tell dad that you're fucking all of your suspects before you bring them in," she spat before leaving out of the room.

Shannon rubbed two fingers on both temples trying to gain a sense of what just occurred. The mastermind Jabari seemed to be closer than she expected, and now it was opening up a door between her and Sarah that had been closed for years. Now that the cat was out of the bag. It was time to show Jabari exactly who the true game player was. There was only one way to win, and Shannon was willing to play for keeps. Keep's that place fools like him under a cell instead of inside one.

* * *

Federal Investigation Room #13

Chris Green

The Board vs Detective Pakori
Downtown Sacramento

The large hand on the bowl clock resting above Detective Pakori's head was ticking louder with every second that passed by. At least that is what it felt like as he waited patiently for the supervisor of the board to appear at his hearing with the bureau. The case manager was typing every word that was spoken, and the assistant was already grilling him with the third-degree questions before the official meeting was even able to start.

The moment Patrick Kegg stepped through the double doors and everyone's posture inside the room tightened like a loose booty. His black tailored suit was fitted to perfection, matching the Giorgio Armani dress shoes on his feet. His silky blonde hair was pushed to the side giving him a grand entrance before he took his seat at the rectangular-shaped table. "Sorry for my tardiness everyone. There was a problem down at central, and I wanted to be sure all was handled before we began. Is the polygrapher in today or will that be another wait?" he questioned his case manager.

"Yes sir. The test will be issued Wednesday. We can proceed."

"Alright then," Patrick responded before placing his attention on Detective Pakori. "So Detective, we've been back and forth with this situation for about a year now. The department has reason to believe that you used excessive force against a suspect which resulted in a homicide. From my understanding, you were trying to stop the robbers of this bank?" Patrick assumed from the papers that were sitting in front of him.

Detective Pakori shuffled in his seat when the question was presented. "Yes. On the day of this robbery, I was called at the station for a stick-up in progress. Once I gathered my response team, I headed over to the Northside and placed my team directly in front of the Merchants Bank and Loans. Upon my arrival, I happened to run into these guys making their way out of the facility. One began to open fire on us. A few of my men returned shots, and one of the men was taken down on the scene while the others were able to flee. That kinda sums it up." Detective Pakori shrugged as if he really didn't want to keep reliving the same drastic moment over again. It was tough to make the decision he did, and never, not once did he think the bureau would be at his doorstep knocking with an iron fist.

Patrick Kegg rubbed his stubby grey goatee, his eyes studied Pakori to see If he could find any slight fault. "Okay, but what I would like to know is why you shot the suspect again once he hit the ground?"

"It was never my intention to murder anyone. I served justice equally and according to the state of law. I am an officer-"

"You broke the code of law when you used excessive force against a man who couldn't oppose a further threat. That's called murder Mr. Pakori, and I'm afraid that our oath doesn't stand behind that. Now my records show that last year around September 3. There was a call about a quadruple homicide in the bounds of Hagginwood. Now the weird thing about that is the guys who we found dead. Johnathan Beasley, better known as Mr. Jubbie. That sounds familiar to you, right? He was the same man you chased and put away for fifteen years. In fact, there was a crew that you couldn't stop fixing your mind against. I'm having a hard time remembering their name." Patrick snapped his fingers repeatedly as if he was thinking hard.

Pakori huffed. "City of Kingz, sir."

"Ah yes. City of Kings. The ultimate crew of destruction who single-handedly took over Sacramento. Those guys. How come out of all these criminals, we happened to find your son inside of one of their gambling spots in critical condition? Not to mention, he was the only survivor that made it out of one of the worst crime scenes I've seen since I began to work with the law."

Pakori stuttered knowing the truth was finally out. Toying with Patrick Kegg was against the rules of the game. He was like the Godfather of The feds, and if he wanted you gone. The rest of the alphabet boys would fall in line with his decision. It was evident that the odds were stacked against him." My son is a sinner, Kegg. He's no different than any other young kid who wants to live the life, but there's a difference. He's actually not made for the streets. He was shot three times during that robbery, and it pained me to reach a crime scene where my son had to be identified as a victim. He was in critical condition for six months where my boy sucked through a straw. These same assholes are the reason I'm sitting right here pleading my case. I'm literally being investigated for a bunch of killers, and bank robbers who forced my hand to do the same job I was given. It's not personal," Pakori stressed.

"Sounds like it to me, sir. I've been doing this for a long time. One shot to the leg forced him down, and the other shot to the back stated that you wanted vengeance on the ones who claimed to be terrorizing Sacramento. For the years that I have known him. The infamous Keyno would never run from a gunfight, especially when it involves the authorities. His rap sheet is filled with aggravated assaults and manslaughters. He's one of the most influential criminals out of the Hagginwood area, and men of his caliber don't change overnight, Pakori."

"What are you trying to say, sir?" He flashed Patrick a curious expression.

"I'm saying that criminals never change Pakori. Kentavious Walker was one of the most ruthless men inside of Sacramento. Which means, if he was trying to harm you, it would've been done and there would be nothing you or the Sacramento Police Department could have done about it. I'll ask again, Detective. Was there any personal beef with you and Kentavious Walker? And if there was, I think it needs to be placed on the table right now or I'm afraid there will be nothing I can do for you when the heads come asking questions?"

Pakori swallowed the hard glob of spit that was lodged in his throat. His expression never changed, and he refused to switch his story when he was so close to knocking down one of the biggest cases in California. "On oath, I, Detective Pakori, state that there was no foul play in the murder of Kentavious Walker."

Flashing him a sinister smile. Patrick Kegg scribbled his signature across the investigation papers and slid his badge and gun back across the desk. "Hopefully, after this investigation hits the board eyes, they agree with you, Pakori because I'm not big on going against my daughter's instincts. She's a professional, and the best at what she does. It's the reason I referred her to your department. Remember that my eyes are everywhere, Pakori. And before you make me look bad, I'll make you cry under a level ten penitentiary for the next sixty-eight years. Have a good day." Patrick stood to go from his seat and headed for the door.

There was a new sheriff in town for the city slickers that was moving recklessly, and Patrick Kegg was ready to enforce his hand, especially when it had something to do with a check being pulled from his pocket. If Pakori wanted to be at the top, he had to earn a spot with the big guys in law enforcement. Unfortunately, Agent Kegg was ready to disintegrate that thought before any bright clues began to frolic in his mind. As he stepped out of the Interrogation room, his eyes landed on the new agent who just joined the bureau. The kid's blonde hair and blue eyes made him fit the image of another genius fed who would rise quickly in the department, but his theory was entirely wrong.

Chris Green

Chapter 6
Village 14
Two Days Later
Sacramento, California

The small block party that was taking place on the street was live-lier than live. Muthafuckas moved around the corners dealing chronic and slanging bags of smack, but the music and food are what kept the energy alive and calm inside of the negative area. Village 14 was never lit like South Hagginwood or Ben Ali, but it did suffice good enough if you needed to find a hood where you could come up.

Jabari sat on the porch of Sip's two-bedroom home listening to Rich the Kid's single cry through the Kenwood speakers. Plug talk had everybody moving like some zombies. The clouds of mariju-ana smoke consumed the parking lot, rising up into the streetlights as if the ground was separating for Doom's day. Leo, Teddy, and Blow bobbed to beat while keeping their eyes glued to the large crowd that surrounded the street.

"So, I'm saying. Did we come here tonight to tighten up our loose screws or are we supposed to be joining the cha-cha slide line?" Blow tooted up his nose with an attitude.

"Yeah, I'm waiting for Sip. His ass ain't got too much longer before I say fuck it and x him out. I don't do sloppy business." Jabari looked around at all the unfamiliar faces.

"Patience guys. It's a virtue." Leo pointed at Sip walking smoothly with a brown-skinned chick through the grass.

His hands were wrapped around her hips and from the look on her face. He was whispering some amazing shit to her. Once he looked up and spotted the crew sitting on his porch, he dismissed his entertainment and put on his game face. Heading up the stairs two at a time, he embraced all of them with a goofy smile. "I see y'all niggas finally stepped out of Hagginwood's comfort zone. I know my trap ain't official like y'all shit, ya smell me? But we still popping for some, baby." He laughed before taking a seat.

Jabari faced him with a disturbing expression. "Listen homie, I don't even know you like that to be sitting in another niggas neighborhood trying to discuss business. We agreed to eleven-thirty, buddy. Not thirty minutes before one. Did you find the other driver or not?"

Teddy, Leo, and Blow moved closer to ensure that no one was tuning in to their conversation.

"No. Well, I mean…I tried… My guy doesn't drive anymore and he's on his family man shit now. Ya dig? Who the hell am I to mess up a happy home?" Sip smiled innocently looking back and forth between them all.

"What type of criminal retires from driving? Did you explain anything to him that's about to occur?" Jabari quizzed.

"Uhhh pretty much."

"And?"

"And he basically told me that he didn't want any part of what we have going on, Jabari. I mean, what the fuck did you expect? You send me to find a driver and offer him a million dollars to be a getaway driver. The numbers alone had that nigga farting, and nervous. He actually thought I was trying to kill him," Sip explained truthfully.

"Damn!" Blow folded his arms roughly in anger. "How in the fuck are we gonna do this in three days if we ain't got the nigga with the wheels?"

"Just calm down. There's a bigger world with better drivers. We just have to get that through Jabari's head." Leo looked down at his best friend with sincerity "Bro, you know what we have to do. He's our last option, but you also know that he's our best option."

Jabari forced a mug on his face. "Who?" His eyebrow was raised like The Rock from the W.W.E.

"Brandon," Teddy answered for him.

"Fuck no!" Jabari jerked his head the opposite way like the conversation wasn't up for debate.

Teddy moved closer to Jabari placing a hand on his shoulder. "Look, Bossman. I'm not trying to be the one that rubs any bullshit in ya face, but you were the same one who wanted him to get away from Ronald. That was his father bro. The one who had the responsibility of taking care of the kid. Once he left, and you took on the role of being his provider, that also meant you took the agreement of teaching him how to be a man also. He watches everything you do and soaks it up like a sponge, Bari. How can you want him to do right if you're doing the same shit to place food in his mouth? I'm not saying just let him run wild to be a whole killer out this muthafucka, but at least allow him to do what he does best. At least he could be earning his own in the process. No matter how hard you wanna keep him away. It's only a matter of time before he breaks loose with you and gets in the mix on his own. Then you would really have to worry. Just think on it, bro. This is the move of our life. You said you wanted out of Cali, and Hagginwood for good. This is it."

Jabari was sure to listen and evaluate everything Teddy said, but the sound of his brother being placed into the streets by his own hands was a hard decision to force. He was overprotective enough, and it would crush his soul to pieces if Brandon happened to be hurt on a job. That would be the day that he never forgave himself.

Leo bending down in front of him broke his trance. "Aye, bro. I see you not really here. Are you sure this needs to be the topic right now?"

"I'm fine," he lied quickly.

"Well, if you're good then we need to be making some serious ass choices Bari. I hate to say it, and no matter how much I feel this nigga is gay or jacked off more times than he's gotten pussy. I have to agree with Teddy. I've never seen anyone drive better than Brandon in my life. My dad drove rigs for a living, so whipping is easy. Your little brother should've been a damn NASCAR driver. I know it's hard bro, but we need him," Leo admitted.

Exhaling heavily, Jabari took his small drink of Pineapple Cîroc to the head and slammed it against the table in defeat. "Since y'all niggas just got this shit figured out. Who's gonna be the one who ensures he makes it back? Who's gonna make sure he doesn't catch that bullet? Because it damn sho ain't about to be neither one of you niggas. That's my champ. He's all I got left, bro. I don't wanna risk him."

"But you risk him every day out here playing with your life. How can you say that you love him, and any day you could be gone yourself?" Teddy shook his head, headed off for the coolers and old cougars.

The statement was a low blow, but it was damn sure the truth. It wasn't a day that didn't go by that Jabari didn't plot or plan to tear a bank's mouth out in order to survive another year. So much was going on, he didn't even realize Brandon was nearly a dropout. The money. The clothes, drugs, or maybe even the influence of what they could do intrigued him to be around. No matter how much he forced him to stay inside, or away from the team. He began to gain a closer bond. Risking his life was a hard decision, but Keyno forced him to grow up the same way. Through experience.

"I'm scared, Leo. He's my little brother." His eyes showed the genuine love he shared for his blood.

"I know Brodie, but this is the way we feed our young one. If we stop, it all stops. This is the last move before we can finally stamp ourselves Kingz of this city. We ain't been stopped yet, so we damn sho ain't about to start having doubt now. We have each other, and no matter what, we all walking away from that shit together. That's a promise I can make on my life." He placed a hand over his chest.

It took a minute for him to adjust to the decision. Choices in the life of the game had to be taken wisely, and Jabari knew that one false move always placed a nigga under the bus. Even though he didn't want to see that happen. The money still had to be made.

"Fine, but all I can do is ask him. If he doesn't agree, it's over," Jabari authorized before standing to his feet to leave.

"You know damn well Brandon ain't passing up shit dealing with a G spot and a steering wheel." Leo chuckled.

"Now that's what I'm not about to take care of. No babies needed," he replied before turning to Blow who leaned against the guard post. "Look, my nigga. I know shit ain't all buttercream with us, but you gotta stop trying to force shit. You're a part of the team, which means you have a voice also. It just doesn't rule over mines." He smirked.

Blow smiled devilishly. "Mhmm. I thought you weren't the boss-type?"

"Only when I need to be, fool. See, that's what's wrong with y'all older niggas today. Y'all wanna be the boss so much that you start bossing the boss around. We gotta remember we're still employed and not the owners of nothing. You can't own ya own until ya free. That's what Jay-Z said, ain't it?" Jabari said walking off.

"I don't know. Never listened to too many East coast niggas. Be sure to check in and let me know where the next meeting is Bossman," Blow yelled with humor.

"McKinley Park. Tomorrow in the morning. Don't be late," Leo answered for him before the two of them headed down the parking lot to Jabari's parked Durango.

Blow watched as he and Leo climbed in the whip and took flight. The small smile that was plastered on his face formed slowly into a frown. The hatred for his coworker was definitely a feeling he despised. Niggas who was on his bad side always happened to find their way into a casket, or creek. The way shit was playing. He knew that soon there was gonna be a confrontation. One that needed order, and he was damn sho gonna make sure that he was the first one in line to see the arrogant bastard Jabari get spanked.

Heading to the back where the drinks were stored. Teddy sat on the wooden porch bench with a thick chick who looked like she was old enough to be his grandmother. Blow couldn't help but shake his head at the thirsty nigga. He would fuck anything with a soft spot between the legs. Old, young, shittt…he would even snatch up the ugly ones on a bad day. The one thing he knew for sure, Teddy wasn't going to leave that party until he had someone walking behind him.

Blow walked slowly over to the section and interrupted his smooth ass convo. "Hey, Ms. Lady. You looking all scrumptious and whatnot. Just to go ahead and cut the small talk, my brother wants you in his bed tonight." He grabbed her hand forcing her to stand from between his legs.

"Umm, how you know I wanna do that?" She grinned from ear to ear.

"Because. You have an ass like a twenty-year-old. Every older woman I know with a lot of ass love it stroked and rubbed. Make sure you wait for him in the front. If you don't mind, I need to speak with him privately," Blow whispered with a wink.

"Mhmmm. I don't wait long Teddy bear, so please don't make me change my mind." Ma dukes walked off with her booty slanging like a wild belt beating the kid's ass.

Once she was out of sight. Teddy frowned. "Goddamn Dr. Os-ley. I like having small interacting sessions before I test out my product, Blow."

"Fuck all that. The bitch going home with you. Jabari agreed but I could tell by his posture, and tone that something still ain't sitting right."

"What you mean? He agreed, right? That's what we wanted, bro."

"Yeah, it is. But something is telling me that it's not gonna hap-pen like that. If you ask me, I say we stick to the plan we came up with and let it fly how it fly," Blow suggested with a crooked eye. He was trying to check Teddy's temperature about making a move against Jabari. The discussion was held a few times between the two when they were alone, but tonight was the moment he needed an answer. Whatever statement came from his mouth would tell him exactly how he needed to handle it all after their last conver-sation.

"Man, you know this still our boy. Why can't we just stress how you feel and make him bust the profit down the middle with us? Jabari has always been good to me, Blow. I've been pondering on that shit and I'm trying to stay level headed with this whole thing." Teddy huffed with exhaustion.

Blow twisted his face and sat down next to him. "Bro, you sound like a whole bitch. The man doesn't give a damn about us. If it's not Leo or Brandon, it's irrelevant. You've been getting un-dercut since we started laying shit down with this man. You don't want yo' own paper. This is the time. Just like we found this lick, he can run across another one. Twenty million isn't the average number of cash a nigga striking for on the daily. I'm talking 'bout cash that can set us straight for life. Twenty million Teddy." Blow shoved his shoulder lightly.

"Yeah, I hear you. Man, twenty million is a lot of money. I just don't want shit to get ugly ya know. Jabari ain't shit to be played with Blow. I'll have to relocate, and literally, never speak to. a nigga I call my brother. All about some paper?" Teddy held open his hands as if the tragedy was already taking place.

"The paper is the small part idiot. Y'all are robbers, not lovers. You take, and the only thing Jabari can do when he finds out is to respect the game like Meek Mill said. It's not like we about to kill the nigga. We taking the paper, leaving him a cut, and heading out of Sacramento to start over. Easy, but I'm not gonna act like I don't need yo, help. Eight million apiece for us both. Who gives a fuck about what comes behind it when I can get rid of you and anyone else that's coming with ya?" Blow stated arrogantly before grabbing a Heineken out of the cooler.

Teddy pulled a joint from behind his ear, sparked it, and inhaled deeply. Eight million dollars definitely sounded sweet to his ears, and the money was surely well needed. Jabari's face continued to pop in his vision as he pondered on Blow's request. Blowing out a cloud of smoke, he turned to look him square in the eyes. "I'm down, but I don't want shit to happen to him or Brandon period. Either that or I'll just have to pass," he bargained, hoping that Blow didn't get too aggressive about the issue.

"Mann that's my word, lil bro. No one is about to get hurt, period. We the ones who are getting the fuck out of dodge. If anything, this same nigga you ready to spare will probably be placing a ticket on your head fifteen minutes after we strike. If you know better, you will follow me down to Florida to my people's spot. We can shack up down there until we get all our shit in order. It's better than moving around sloppy. You just gotta trust me, lil bro," Blow beckoned with a brotherly tone.

"I trust you, bro. I trust you. Let's just hurry and get this shit over with," Teddy said, standing to his feet.

Blow followed suit and embraced him into a firm hug. "Mark my words. You're gonna be thanking me when we're at the beach chilling in the Bahamas in a few weeks. The city belongs to us, including the rest of this shitty ass world."

"Big facts." Teddy grinned. "Now if you don't mind, I got a mean date with Mama Harris' big booty self. She and I finna get acquainted like the Weeknd and Selina Gomez."

Laughing, Blow patted his back. "You drove down here yourself my guy. I got my ride. Handle the business, and make sure you're down at McKinley Park in the morning. Bright, and early."

"Gotchaaa!" Teddy threw the thumbs up and headed straight for the thick, and red woman waiting by his car door.

"Don't be fucking late!" Blow shouted before shaking his head at the retard. He knew with Teddy's help; it would be easier to track the movements and decisions Jabari was bound to make. Nobody was able to know a person better than a best friend who stuck with you twenty-four seven. The chess pieces were falling along well on the board. Now it was time to set his Queen in effect to protect him permanently. There could only be one King of the City and losing was not pondering through Blow's mind for one second. It was time to show a young nigga how a real taker got down. It was either cross or be crossed.

Chris Green

Chapter 7
McKinley Park 8:12 A.M.

Pulling his whip down in the section of the large, empty parking lot. Teddy parked his rental and climbed out soaking in the bright sun as it pinched at his skin. The breeze was brisking lightly through the air., and he could spot Jabari, Brandon, and Leo sitting at the other end of the lot like they were waiting for a Fast and Furious shoot. Their cars were parked sideways, and the sound of a loud motor behind him caused his head to jerk back. Sip's Audi A7 was howling past him doing over 100 miles an hour. The wind along from his vehicle nearly forced Teddy to fall against the concrete. Being sure to hold his fitted hat down. He held his breath until the vibration of his car bypassed. Sip came to a screeching halt directly in front of the team.

"That was forty-three seconds flat. I've never seen a bitch beat that because today is my first time." He smiled stepping out of the luxury sports car.

Jabari nodded. "That sounds good, but I have to see it in action. Race him," he ordered nodding his head towards Jabari.

Leo agreed with a huge smile, and by the time Teddy reached them. It was already stamped. In order for Brandon to make the cut, he had to knock Sip out of the box.

"Man, you almost killed me with that damn car. You can't be speeding in a public area like this fool. I'm still a citizen motherfucker!" Teddy shook his head before sitting on top of Jabari's hood.

"Which one do you want Brandon?" Leo asked, pointing at their test cars that were lined up beside each other.

Brandon didn't get a chance to choose before Jabari tossed a set of keys to the 96 Gray Corvette.

"But Bari. I don't know how to-"

"Ahh hell nah, Brandon, Mr. Best Driver these niggas ever seen. Get ya ass in the seat, sir." Sip laughed before hopping back in his Audi. After watching Brandon take his precious ass time to climb in his whip, he knew the race was over.

Leo made his way in front of their cars with his hands held high. "The rules are simple fellas. Don't hit shit, especially each other. I want a full circle around the park until you reach the back of Jabari's Durango. The first one to pass us up again wins. Understood?" He looked at them both before taking a few steps back.

Brandon sat inside of the Corvette with a dumbfounded expression. Not only was the seat uncomfortable, but it was an automatic shift. Some shit that Brandon didn't like to operate. Before the race could even begin, he could feel the momentum of his loss building up. Once Leo held one finger up, the boys mashed down in their gas pedals allowing their engines to rev loudly. Brandon was sure to keep his eyes open without a single blink. Just as Leo flagged his arms, the two of them mashed off leaving a trail of smoke and tire marks behind them. The corvette Brandon was pushing got off to a great start, but it wasn't the whip that he was used to controlling. The sound of Sip's Audi creeping forced him to look in the rearview mirror. Just as he hit the first corner, Sip was directly on his bumper bending it next to him. Their cars were so close they could've shaken hands through each other's windows. Refusing to let up, Brandon mashed down on the gas trying to place a small distance between them. The horsepower inside of the engine was only so strong, and by the time they reached the second corner. Sip's car was creeping past him swifter than a mouse. The small lead that Brandon thought was his eventually turned into a steep distance from the high-powered motor inside of the vehicle he was going against. Feeling himself falling too fast behind. He floored his gas pedal to try and catch back. The last corner was approaching, and fast. Once they reached the edge, Sip drifted smoothly around the curb as if he already practiced this shit thirty times. Brandon turned his steering wheel to the far left trying to contain the car, but still ended bumping roughly into the guard rail. The skills he acquired allowed him to get the corvette back on track, but by the time he cleared the corner, Sip was already coming to a halt in front of Jabari's bumper of his whip. The crew waited in silence until he pulled his whip past the finish line. Blow was already laughing his guts out from the salty look on Brandon's face. Once they stepped out of the cars to meet in the center, Sip smiled. "This is my world, lil bro. You need a little more experience, kid."

"Bullshit nigga. That's an automatic. It's weak as fuck. I wanna race again. This time I want that car." He pointed over to the all-white Shelby Mustang 500.

"That shit. You wanna race my Audi against this old ass piece of metal. You might as well sign my name on ya shirt and give up now." Sip smacked his lips, with a confident grin.

Jabari sat in silence when his little brother pulled a wad of cash from out his right front pocket. He could see the anger inside of him about losing, and now the competition was really on. Whether he knew it or not. The race was his interview for a job, and at the moment he wasn't making the cut regardless of being little bro or not.

"How much you got on it then nigga?" Brandon tossed five crispy hundreds on top of Jabari's car.

Sip matched his money, and through his own bucks on top of the hood. "It wouldn't matter what whip you pick Brandon. I'm the best in Sacramento, baby boy. Eat the dust and let me know what it tastes like when we make it back around."

Ignoring his fake ass scare tactic. Brandon climbed inside of the Shelby Mustang and started the engine. The hungry motor sounded like it was ready to tear the pavement from the ground and to make it even better. It was a stick shift. The perfect toy for a real car driver. Lining up at the mark, Leo stepped back in front of the boy's cars. "Same thing fellas. This time. It ain't no do-overs. Whoever wins, operates the getaway team. Period," he stated.

Waiting for the signal again. Brandon stared at Leo's hand eagerly waiting for it to fall. This time shit was going a little different. Not only was a race on the line, but the chance of working along the side of his brother forced him to get his head in the race. Just as Leo dipped his hand. Brandon was smashing down on the gas, causing his car to lift a few inches off the ground. The race was back on. Both engines howling for dear life to be released. The cars matched evenly nose to nose until the first corner appeared. Being sure not to be outshined again. Brandon grabbed the far-left corner and began turning before the curb was near. The heavy-duty mustang swerved tilting slightly to the side. Sip had to make a wider turn in order for the two cars not to clash. Brandon still didn't panic, and once he gained control of the mean machine. He leveled it back down on all fours. The speed of Sip's Audi continued to pace directly next to him, but the solid big block engine was pushing Brandon faster down the bumpy concrete. The doors to his car were rattling like a bass drum, and the next turn was directly ahead. The slight mash on his brakes allowed Sip to slide his small rocket around the corner. Once his face reached Brandon's window. He flicked a bird and started to accelerate. Brandon kicked the mustang into fourth gear, and the speed finally began to pick up. The rearview mirror was shaking so hard that he felt if he pushed any further. The entire car would fall apart. Once his eyes connected with the last turn. He made a small prayer and tested the water. Kicking his whip into fifth gear. He placed the pedal to the medal. The speedometer started to rise, and the short distance that Sip had was hawked back down immediately. The large turn allowed Brandon to drift his big duty Shelby around the edge like a cat running from a wild dog. His bumper slightly tapped SIP's front bender allowing him to take the lead again. Once Brandon spotted his opportunity to bring it home. He slammed his foot down letting the beauty purr with a vengeance. By the time he was able to slow down. He was more than forty-eight feet away from the finish line. Sip's Audi was just passing the mark when he looked back to see that the race was far from over.

"Yeaahhhh! I told you bitch." He laughed to himself before throwing the car in reverse. Sliding back to where his older brother and friends stood, he rolled down the window, grinning from ear to ear. Placing the Shelby in park. Brandon stepped out of the car and snatched his stack off the hood of Jabari's Durango. "As I said nigga, you can claim that shit about being the best only when I'm not around."

"You got a lucky one in. That's all. I got all day. We got some bigger space on the outskirts too. Straight road," Sip offered. He wasn't furious about the loss, but he damn sure wasn't happy with a blowout against his Audi. Still in all, he had to give credit to where it was due. Out of everyone he raced behind the wheel. The young champ was the nicest with the whip game. Hands down.

"Maybe some other time. That's only if Jabari doesn't care." He placed his attention on his big brother.

"Let's handle the business first champ. You did good." He wrapped an arm around his neck, jerking him in a playful manner.

Leo walked over to them both with a fat ass smile. "See what I mean? All this time we have been losing out on having the perfect getaway, and you been holding him hostage in the house. Was that enough proof that he's ready?"

Sip and Teddy stood to the side quietly waiting for his answer. It was enough pressure with not having all the pieces for their mission in order. Now that it was coming together. The ball was in Jabari's hand. After taking a small moment of silence to himself. He gazed at his team nodding slowly. "Alright. He can drive."

"Yesss!" Leo yelled with excitement.

"It's about damn time. I could've told you that he was going to dust Sip slow ass. That boy is a young Jimmie Johnson," Teddy added with a yawn.

"Are you serious, bro? I really can come with you now?" Brandon stared into Jabari's eyes with a straight face.

Even though he wanted to deny him so badly, he handled his business fair and square. There was no way to exclude him from the action any longer. "Yeah, Champ. You get to ride with the crew. Only on one condition."

The fellas grew quiet knowing that Jabari obviously had something else up his sleeve. Before he spoke, he pulled a fresh chain from his front pocket. It was the exact same one that Keyno gave him before he died. It was an exact replica. Placing it on Brandon's neck, he smiled. "Promise to always follow me and you'll win, and never allow money to lead you the wrong way. Never," Jabari said with emphasis.

"I promise, bro. That's my word." His face glowed up while the small diamonds danced around his neck. "It's just like the one you got, minus the diamonds. How much did you pay for this?"

"It doesn't matter. It's yours, and you will never be limited to anything if you listen and pay attention. This game is deadly, and it's not what I planned out for your future, but in the end, You're growing to make your own decisions. You will follow all rules and get back in school in order to stay on the move with the team. Is that understood?" Jabari asked with an inquisitive eye.

"Yeah, bro." He smiled before wrapping him into a tight hug. "Thanks for giving me a chance, Bari. I swear I won't let you down, man."

Rubbing two knuckles across Brandon's head, Jabari laughed. "You better not or I'ma have to replace ya. We don't fuck up, champ."

"Oh, trust me, we all have had our fuck up days... Shittt, I had to be a nasty slut president for six months and wasn't nobody stressing that." Teddy shrugged, opening up his car door to grab the blunt from his ashtray.

"Once again fatty, that's because you naturally have hoe tendencies. It wouldn't be right if you were appearing to be a man with a pair of balls. They actually might call out your full government and fuck us all over." Leo laughed.

"Hardy har-har motherfucker. I still get more ass than a mattress. And if being a nasty bitch means M's in my pocket, cut this dick off!" Teddy yelled before starting his car. Kendrick Lamar's song, *Backseat Freestyle* was beating the paint off his shit and of course, the tinted windows made him even more of a target for the police department. But as usual, Teddy was gonna be a bitch about whatever, and the crew was cool with that. He was a natural, loveable, fat ass. The one who could get away with eating all the Fruity Pebbles on a Friday morning friend. Jabari knew that no matter what he accomplished growing up, he placed together one of the best teams in the world. He just prayed that their ambition and loyalty rose more as they continued to grind and shine. Sacramento was officially looking at the new City of Kingz.

Chris Green

Chapter 8
Strawberry's House
Old Sacramento Townhomes

The last episode of "Snowfall" was airing, and the air conditioning was pumping harder than a bitch on a ten-inch rod. Strawberry was balled up under her comforter with her hands buried between her thighs. Boredom had struck again and now she was on her third drama TV series for the day. Her phone was dry as fuck, and everything that scrolled across her flatscreen was advertising the lamest shit ever about relationship statuses. After scrolling through three hundred channels on the Comcast box, Strawberry's doorbell sounded off once, forcing her to climb out of her comfortable position. Her Dior booty shorts hugged her ass with a snug fit, and the Guess halter top she wore was bust slightly down the middle, exposing a nice amount of her cleavage. Before her guest could ring the doorbell again, she opened it. Her grin started to spread when she laid eyes on Jabari standing on her doorstep. He was dressed in a nice Louis Vuitton button-down shirt. His white slacks were tailored, and the white Dior sneakers he wore complimented his entire outfit. His beard and tapeline were hit up, and he couldn't help but flash her that coochie getting ass smile. He was magnificent in every way through her eyes. A young man who was destined to be a true boss. The only thing she couldn't get him to see was the loyalty of her being the right one for him. No matter how much sex, no matter how the feelings got poured out, he would always remain the same and continue to encourage her to date and mingle. She wanted to be more than just friends, and the addiction for him was growing more by the day.

"Hey boy." she snickered leaning in for a hug. She was sure to let him see all that ass jiggling behind her.

If it was one thing he couldn't resist, it was her sex game. Strawberry was the ultimate freak when it came to showing Jabari that she could please him. That was the one thing that scared him when it came down to their friendship. For some reason, he always ended up back in front of her doorstep looking for something to speak about or asking miscellaneous questions that could've been spoken about over the phone. Those small interactions always led to her face down, ass up, and getting her pussy pounded until she released one of the best orgasms a bitch could ever stress about busting. He was a fetish that couldn't be scratched, and she actually loved it.

"Wassup Berry? What you got going, ma?" He held her waist, looking down into her seductive pupils. His tongue would rub across his smooth lips every time she moved her hips in a different direction. She knew that was a major enticer for him, and Strawberry was always willing to play the game. "What are you doing here Jabari? I barely see you, so this is a shocker." Her small hand was mounted against her hip like she was demanding an answer.

"I was in the neighborhood and wanted to come to talk to you. Can I come in?" he asked like that shit was really about to get denied.

Tooting up her lips, she grabbed him by the shirt, pulling him inside. Closing the door behind them. She applied the locks and walked over to the couch taking a seat beside him. "So, what you up to? I haven't seen ya ass in almost a month, so don't hit me with one line to try and sum it up."

Jabari chuckled and rubbed her thigh. "I've been moving around establishing a few things. Trying to start a few businesses, and of course, making the mula. Still in all, I was thinking about you and I felt like it couldn't wait," he admitted.

Strawberry's eyes lowered trying to see what he had up his sleeve, but of course, he was moving like a jet li nigga so it was

72

never no telling where Jabari's mind could go. "What's going on, Is there something wrong?"

Lowering his vision, he tried to block out her gaze, knowing the moment was hard as fuck for him to handle. Strawberry placed a finger under his chin, forcing him to lift his head. Her expression was now cold like a block of ice. "Jabari, what's going on? Speak to me, now," her tone was sterner.

"I don't think I can come around you anymore, Strawberry. I have to leave and get some space because I feel that what we're doing is getting too serious," he mumbled, not really wanting to explain the truth. At the time.it was impossible, and one true statement would only open up a door for a thousand more questions.

Strawberry's face balled in anger from his remark. "Excuse me. What the hell are you talking about Jabari? I haven't done anything for you to stay away from me. Where is this coming from? Is it Victoria?" she spat.

"No, it's not Victoria. It's me. I'm getting too attached to you, Strawberry. I have a lot going on and right now I don't need anything falling back on the ones I care for. My respect for you is on a thousand, and no, I'm not doing this just to break things off with you. I'm doing it to better you," he admitted.

"Better me? Nigga, I sit in this bitch drawling over you all day Jabari. It's hours that go by where I can't think about nothing or no one but you. What did I do? I said I respect your relationship. I understand I'm not your woman, but you ain't gotta do this. Is someone forcing you to stop dealing with me? What is it?" she pleaded, trying to get him to keep eye contact.

"It's not you. It's me. I'm starting to get too attached, and I don't wanna hurt you. It's not right Strawberry. It's not fair to Victoria either?"

Huffing lightly, she laughed off his remark. "Look, Jabari. I know that you have a lot going on so I can understand you needing a break to handle your business baby boy, but go acting like you never coming back or something. I mean what are you really saying?" She folded her arms preparing to hear the worse.

Instead of going back, and forth, he leaned over, placing a delicate kiss on her lips. Their tongues slowly began to intertwine when he placed a hand gently around her throat. Jabari could feel her body quivering under his grasp. She was trembling with ecstasy pumping through her inner thighs, and the way her eyes rolled clearly showed him that he was in full control. Strawberry was more than just a friend. She was close like family. Not only did she teach him most of the shit he knew between the sheets, but she schooled him on a lot of things that were occurring in the streets. Sacramento wasn't the average neighborhood to become a superstar or the next top athlete, but it was a drug dealer on every corner. And if you didn't have relatives to help you along the way, there was always a street gang ready to initiate you in three hundred and sixty-five days out of the year. Her spirit was more like an aunt, but every time his eyes and hands laid against her skin, all that shit flew clean out of the window.

As Jabari slowly pulled the shirt over her head, she stared at him seductively. Her body was loose as glue, and nothing could ever stop her from letting him have his way. He was so young, but his spirit was much older and stronger. His hands caressed Strawberry's lower back before he began sucking on her neck. He lightly flicked his tongue across her earlobe causing her pussy to thump with anticipation. Their lips met again, locking passionately as if they would never see each other after that night. His hands roamed down to her plump behind, squeezing it lightly. She released a pleasant moan. "Ssss…daddy."

Jabari stood to his feet and removed his shoes. Next, his shirt, and right after, he unbuckled his pants letting them drop to the floor. The Givenchy boxers on his backside exposed his huge print forcing Strawberry to slide her itty-bitty shorts from her ass. Her smooth skin glowed to perfection and not a scratch roamed down her body. From her hair to the nails, and even the feet, she still was spectacular. A sight that a man who dreams of seeing. It was the same reason Jabari had such a hard time staying away from her. The dimples in her cheeks poked out with every smile she mustered. Her Purple berry scented lotion enticed him so much that his mouth began to water. Wasting no time, he spread her legs staring at the pretty prize. It was perfection in plain sight. A heart-shaped kitty that was pulsating as if the wrong action could make it explode. Watching him lick his lips twice, she knew what was about to come next. Before she could close her eyes and lean back, Jabari was feasting away. His nasty slurping sounds always forced her to fidget. He didn't just lick the pussy. He nibbled, sucked, and even bit that motherfucker sometimes when he was in that steamy ass mode. It was rare, but it was damn sure the due date because he was putting it down. Every time Strawberry raised her head, she would watch his fat tongue slide up and down the crease of her cookie. Locking her love button between his lips, he rubbed her stomach and sucked viciously demanding for her to flash that sexy ass fuck face. Sure enough, she was folding, grinding, and crying from the satisfaction he was applying, and letting up was not in his vocabulary. He caressed her thighs gently making sure he gave all the pleasure possible. Once he felt her legs shake, he knew that juice was about to erupt from her sweet spot. Sucking as if his life depended on it, he tasted her nectar filling his tongue with delight. Fuck Bubblicious, Strawberry was a Fruit Gusher. Jabari grabbed her ass and locked her down until he received all of her offerings.

Wiping his mouth with a backhand, a sneaky smile formed across his face. She was heaving harder than a bitch. Her body was sweating lightly, nipples were hard as pebbles, and her fingers didn't hesitate to massage that pussy waiting for her next surprise.

All she could stare at was his weapon that stood at attention through his expensive boxer briefs. Slowly dropping them down, his shit dropped out like it was bombs over Baghdad. His precum was dripping lightly from the tip, and the sight alone forced her to shudder.

Stroking his piece a few times, he bit on his bottom lip. "Do you want it?" he whispered.

"Please daddy. I need it," she begged, tapping her kitty with an open hand.

Taking a step back, he strolled smoothly towards the hallway leading to the back before he crossed the threshold. He looked back at her panting profusely. Her lips quivered wanting to speak, but she couldn't find the words she needed to explain how much he was driving her insane. Before she could say anything. He smirked. "Rule number one. When you see the man heading for the shower, you follow ma." He teased and stroked his masterpiece one last time for her before disappearing to the bathroom.

Massaging her clit with two fingers. She stood from the couch and made her way back to the pain room. The shower was his safe haven to beat the pussy however he chose, and she had every intention of letting him fill her up. Entering the steamy bathroom, she stared him down as he let the water caress against his chiseled chest and abs. His wavy hair was glowing under the showerhead, and his eyes never blinked as he watched her walk slowly towards him. Stepping inside, she grabbed a hold of his dick and gripped it with authority.

"Mama 'bout to suck this motherfucka dry. Keep your eyes on me, and if you don't beat this pussy after I'm done, this shit will start all the way back over, nigga," she ordered before spitting on his shaft nastily. Taking him into her mouth, She gagged until she could feel her eyes tear up. Her head began to bob with ease. Slobber dribbled lightly down her right cheek and she still didn't stop serving her order. After feeling him reach her tonsils, she pulled him out of her mouth to catch a breather. "You're not leaving. Do you hear me?" she demanded.

All Jabari could do was nod in compliance. He knew that she wasn't about to let up, and after she stuffed him back down her throat. It clarified that their night was definitely gonna be a long one.

Chris Green

Chapter 9
Las Vegas, Nevada
M.G.M Casino
10:13 P.M.

The bright lights inside of the huge M.G.M. Casino glowed at a distance. Not only was it a busy night for the tellers, and dealers, but the special performance from Arianna Grande and Bruno Mars was causing the building to become overcrowded by the minute. Leo stood in the mirror inside of the men's bathroom observing his appearance. Besides the long set of dreads and incapability to move around the Casino with expertise, Leo could have surely gone for the Chief of Security. His hair was wrapped in a set of kinky twists. The red workers' vest Veronica provided him with allowed him to blend right in with the other employees that were on the casino floor. His walkie-talkie was tuned in to every channel making sure to tune in on all the action that was going on inside the building, and just his luck, the casino was in need of extra workers that were willing to be paid under the table due to excess crowds. He never had to attend the small interview that the rest was dragged through thanks to his Italian princess. She was sure to cover every ground that he needed in order for their mission to go smoothly. The job was pretty easy. All Leo had to do was make his way towards the casino's safe, which was stored behind the security booth. Once he was able to get past that, the rest was gonna be sweet as pie. The only problem was the armed guards standing post at the east wing hallway which was the route he needed to take in order to reach the security section. A fifteen-man Las Vegas Police crew was already guarding the building, and the facility was laced with two cameras on each corner. Every floor needed to be accessed by the elevator keeper who stood post with a key card twenty-four seven. After he would put in work to get past the security crew, the mission would officially begin ticking. One thing Leo was positive about was his grade average damn sure wasn't a 3.8 for nothing. Today that shit was about to be put to use. It was time to show the Sin City that Sacramento raised official takers also. Now, it was just a matter of timing.

Making sure his suit was on point with the fake I'd badge he designed himself, he headed straight for the east wing corridor. It took at least ten minutes to walk around the casino and reach the sectioned off area. It was off-limits to certain people. Let's just say, if your bank account wasn't laced with about seven zeros, you were bound to be arrested and hauled off to jail. Management barely let certain employees cross the east wing, so if Leo was gonna make it count. It was all gonna have to be on the first shot. Making his way around the corner, two big bulky police officers stood post in front of the stairs that led down to the security floor, and treasury.

Once they spotted him walking forward, one of the men placed a hand on his shoulder. "Hey, sir. What are you blind or just plain stupid? Read the sign." He pointed to the wall where a white poster was marked with a stencil. It read: *Management only!! No exceptions.*

Leo looked down at the strong ass hand that was resting on his shoulder and chuckled. "If you don't mind, I'll be needing this shoulder for the next forty years or so. Yo shit feels like a building leaning against me, bro. And what's the big deal about the management sign if I was sent back here to handle something for the authorities at the front desk?"

The other black police officer laughed. "Yeah right. What authority? We've been running this shit by ourselves for the past two weeks. All the men with authority are already down these steps sitting behind us, little man," he confirmed.

"Uhh, I wouldn't say that. See, I was just hired by this guy and according to the clerk at the register, Mr. Jackson, definitely has authority. In fact. I think he's looking to hire a group of new security guards. I mean being that he knows my father who made a tremendous endorsement with Mr. Jackson for their resort business. After that clears, I would officially be the head manager of M.G.M myself. He's only a phone call away. It shouldn't take but a second to find him." Leo waved them off and acted as if he was speaking through his walkie talkie. "This is Leon Jackson. Uncle Jack, can you please come in? I repeat Uncle Jack, can you turn your radio to channel three please?"

Before he could get a response, one of the Las Vegas Police Officers tapped him on the shoulder. "Hey big man, it's just a small mistake. No need to pull him away from any business to straighten something so small, right?" he suggested as if that shit was good enough for an apology.

"Hmm. I'm not sure, sir. You tell me. My uncle owns lots of property around this area and before anyone can tell me how to do my job, you might need to find out who all you're working around first. You get rid of that ugly hat, it makes your uniform look tacky, and you," Leo pointed towards the swoll black officer. "You have five days to lose seventy-eight pounds or you will not be working at any casino on this strip. Remember that my name is Leon Jackson and my family nearly owns all of this shit. So, before you lose your blessings and occupation, try staying quiet and do what you're paid to do."

"Yes sir." They both nodded in unison before stepping out of his way.

Giving them a crooked eye, Leo shook his head and continued down the flight of stairs. The steel door that sat at the bottom was mounted to the wall, and it automatically opened once he stepped a certain amount of feet in front of it. The long hallway sitting behind the closed-off section was bigger than the opposite side that he was standing on. Numerous rooms aligned against the hallway, some with transparent mirrors and some with black tinted windows. A few people moved about with envelopes of cash in their hands not paying him any attention and the smell of fresh bills was definitely lingering through the air. Stopping in front of a black window that was titled coins, Leo placed his face against the glass. Feeling stupid for even trying the stunt, he wiggled the doorknob and still came up short. It was locked.

"Hey! What the fuck are you doing down here, man? This isn't a section for red vests." A medium-size Italian man stood in the center of a doorway with a crazed look. Turning around to face him, he recognized that it was a full Italian family reunion in the room behind him. Their faces were lost as if they only knew the words kill and capisce. One of the men who were standing was an exact replica of the man who was standing at the door confronting Leo. Obviously, it was the wrong time to be a different race and too many Black Lives Matter movements had other bitches feeling slimy as a snail. That was an incident he didn't want to be caught in.

"Uh, yes sir. I was looking for Mr. Jackson, the keeper for the sixth floor. He was supposed to come and drop off a few things in security and I happened to get lost trying to find him."

"Well try not to get lost in this area. We don't like animals. They run wild, and we are too organized. Security is towards the front. The back is off-limits. Go." Mikey pointed the opposite way with a stern finger.

"Sure thing," Leo agreed after noticing the look on all the pasta muthafucka faces. He had already seen *Carlito's Way* and *Goodfellas* to know how those bitches rocked and sleeping with the fish damn sho wasn't on his agenda. Making his way back towards the main entrance, he heard the meeting room door close with a light thud. That was his cue to game that shit until he made it. Turning around on a twenty-million-dollar move was absurd, and Jabari wasn't about to place his feet, bows, and knees nowhere across his chin or face because of a fuck up. Spinning in his heels, Leo turned back around and quickly rushed past the room that nearly scared him to death. Once he bent the first left corner, he froze at the sight in front of him. Four rooms were connected together with over fifteen workers counting tons of bills. The cameras were still beaming everywhere, but he had come too far to back out now. The employees continued to do their job by separating large bills, small ones, and coins. There were at least three million dollars that he estimated with his eyes sitting directly behind a glass window in front of him. His knees wanted to buckle, but being a pussy wasn't gonna cut it at the moment. Waking all the way down to the end of the hall. He stared at all the loose cash, and the major jackpot finally popped out of the blind. It was about twenty- six feet tall with a steel door that looked tough as a titanium garbage truck. The lever alone looked as if it weighed at least three hundred pounds. Using his calculations from the top of his head, he eyeballed the diameter and width of the money bank. It was gonna be a hard one, but the connect was sure to bless him with some special toys that don't like the word no. After scoping out all the necessary details, Leo made his way down further until he reached a bathroom area. Quickly pushing inside, he pulled out his cell and dialed Jabari's throwaway line. After a couple of rings, he picked up anxiously.

"Talk to me. Did you get in?"

"Yeah nigga, I did, but I had to get through GI Jack and Goro. Then I crossed paths with some Italians that were filming the *Godfather 8* and nearly got gutted like a fucking fish," he stressed, looking to ensure no one was able to hear or see him. Being sure to look round for any cameras, he moved to one of the stalls and locked himself inside.

"Listen, Jabari. This is a big ass safe. Not to mention that this bitch is flooded with Las Vegas PD, I counted at least sixty guns in this building alone, bro."

"Be easy. That's why I plan for shit like this. I've got the plan. You did your part. Just start the timer and keep me filled on what's going on across your radio. It's time to get paid, nigga," Jabari assured. "Send me the coordinates, and let's make this shit go kaboom, baby."

"Alright. I'm forwarding them to you now. The clock is being set for twenty minutes as we speak, and it's starting now," Leo said before pushing the button. "Aye, Jabari?"

"Yeah wassup, bro?"

"Be careful man," he said sincerely.

"Always man. Stop being gay and put your robbing face back on. When you hear the boom, that's your cue to get the fuck out of there. I don't care whether we make it in or not."

"Gotcha," Leo assured before hanging up the call.

Wiping the small line of sweat from his brow, he looked at his Rolex Submariner watch. Time was now ticking down. Either the next few minutes would bring a large payday or the worst day of his team's life.

* * *

Walking through the dark sewer, Teddy and Blow were sure to keep their guns aimed in front of them. Jabari held the blueprints to the casino in front of him while aiming the flashlight up towards the ceiling. The section he was looking for was slightly difficult to find when they first made their way inside the dirty underground jungle. However, after ten minutes of spinning in the same circle, he suspected that they were now in the right spot according to the document.

"This is it. We got it," Jabari assured, placing his bag on the solid concrete slab that rested on the side of the dirty water bank. "The four corners are facing outwards towards the opposite direction which means that something is mounted on top of it. It's the safe. We got seventeen minutes." Jabari opened the first bag of C4 explosives and handed them carefully to Teddy.

"Shit, what the fuck is that?" Blow yelled, jumping harder than a mutahfucka. "Big ass fucking rat, man."

"Man, you around this bitch cutting niggas open and blowing bitches' brains out, yet you scared of these harmless ass rats, cuz?" Teddy frowned with aggravation lining his tone.

"Man, that shit looks like a damn cat. I ain't use to no shit like that nigga. I'm a clean motherfucker, so me and rats don't get along."

"Right? Try cleaning ya damn vision to focus on what we got going, man. We're working while you jumping, scary-ass nigga," Teddy spat grabbing four more blocks of C4 from the bag.

Jabari turned around snapping his finger in a snappy motion. "Hey man. Can we please get this fucking paper and goof off later on? Teddy, me, and Blow will lift you up, and you're gonna paste all ten blocks around the diameter of that square. The extra ones in the other bags will go directly in the middle to give us a little leverage on the concrete caving in. We need a straight drop on the first try or its plan B," he explained quickly.

"Cool. Let's go." Teddy moved over to the center of the sewer's floor and picked up six blocks of explosives.

In one swift motion, Jabari and Blow lifted him directly under the designated spot for the bombs to be attached. After slapping the first six in place, Blow eased the rest up into his hands. They moved slowly around in a square until every space under their target was covered, easing Teddy back down to the ground. Jabari took a second look at the ceiling and nodded. Pulling out his cell, he called his cleanup crew and received an answer on the first ring. "Yo, what's the read? You want us to take off now?"

"Everything is golden. Royale, right now," he demanded before ending the call. Glancing back at his watch, it was now fourteen minutes clicking down, and it was moving fast. All Jabari could hope for was his second crew to get in the spot, and make that shit happen at that exact second. Time meant everything at the moment, and a second too late could crash all their hard work to the ground.

"So how long we waiting?" Blow tilted his head impatiently.

"Until this phone ring again. Now it's just about the time. We only have so much," he responded. The only thing he wanted to hear was that ringtone, and shit was going up through the roof.

Chapter 10
Casino Royale

The two large Suburbans that pulled in front of Casino Royale came to a screeching halt forcing a few citizens to jump out of the way. Once the doors swung open, five men dressed in Police swat suits spilled out with large assault rifles in their hands. Their half face mask was covering their mouths, and The driver in the vehicles remained inside to ensure they could have their cars secured by the time they returned. Jogging swiftly with their guns to the entrance. People jumped clear out of their path sensing that the officers were on a serious mission. Once they crossed the entrance. One disguised officer removed a large chain from his duffle bag and wrapped it around the front door, placing a master lock around the links. One of the men aimed his Ak47 to the ceiling and let off a rapid amount of shots.

Boccccc!

Bocccccccc!!!

"If you would like to live, instead of dying in the next thirty seconds, you'll drop whatever you're doing and place your faces and hands against the floor," he screamed at the top of his lungs. Numerous bodies began falling and the other three armed men began to run around and relieve all the panicking guards of their weapons.

The boss man in charge, who let off some shells in the air, spotted a clerk teller removing a phone from his pocket. The reaction was so quick that no one expected it to happen. Walking over to the white male, the disguised robber released seven slugs directly into his face, killing him instantly. His body dropped behind the counter allowing his soul to be relieved. His coworker was hiding behind the bottom of the counter with her mouth covered in fear. The sight of her friend's face was shredded in a matter of seconds, and she wasn't trying to be next. Muffling her cries, she kept her back plastered to the wall praying that someone would come in for their rescue.

"Now, I warned all of you sons of bitches to move correctly and you'll be able to be reunited with your families and loved ones tonight. This will only take a second, but if you make me get violent, I'll take it out on everything!" he shouted while shooting a few reckless shots in the air. The quietness assured him that somebody was paying attention. That forced a smile on his face.

The woman behind the counter spotted her friend's phone and slowly reached for it. Trying to be careful not to move sloppy, she slid the bloody phone closer using her feet. Her hands were shaking nervously as she dialed 911 into the pad, pressing dial. The voices of the men could be heard moving around at a distance, and she wasn't trying to raise her head to see anything.

"911, what is your emergency?" the operator answered quickly.

"Ma'am, I'm a card dealer at the Casino Royale and we are being robbed by numerous men. They have weapons, and they murdered my coworker." She sniffled lightly into the receiver.

"Ma'am hold on one second while I transfer your call to the federal authorities. The line clicked and began to ring again. Not even a second later, her call was answered.

"Ma'am, are you there?" a man's voice questioned.

"Yes," she whispered.

"My name is Patrick Kegg with the Federal Bureau of Investigations. You're currently in Casino Royale. These robbers, is there anyone who you can identify? How do these guys look?" he asked, hoping to get a lead.

"I don't know. They have on masks. I'm not sure. They may be young from the sound of their voices," she cried at a low tone.

The arm of one of the robbers snatched her quickly up by the hair, forcing her to drop the phone. She instantly began to scream knowing that she was about to receive brutal treatment as an example. The leader smiled as his associate held the dirty bitch in his grasp. Spotting the cellular phone active on a phone call, he picked it up. "Hello?"

"Who is this?"

"That depends on who this is sir?" the robber replied.

"This is Patrick Kegg with the F.B.I. and you guys are going to be taken down. Help is already on the way, so save yourself and release those innocent people now," he authorized.

Chuckling inside the line, he disconnected the call. "Access denied." He smiled before raising the gun at the woman's head. His partner in crime turned his head in time before her brains exploded from her skull.

Pow!

Exhaling with a smile, the leader of the crew dialed Jabari's number on his own cell. It didn't take long for the line to pick up. "Talk to me."

"Boom-boom, baby." He smirked before hanging up. The sight of police officers and guards running from the M.G.M. across the street. Blue lights were beginning to slide up from every corner and the show was officially about to begin. Sliding his mask over his face, he shouted, "It's showtime boys!"

* * *

Hanging up the phone call, Jabari glanced at his watch one last time. There were only nine minutes left, and everyone was about to be used wisely. Looking at Teddy and Blow, he slid a gas mask over his face. "It's time," he said seriously with a firm clutch on his assault rifle.

Teddy and Blow followed suit by sliding on their mask and sliding to the side of the sewer wall. Jabari stepped back behind a

Chris Green

brick wall and exhaled. Pressing the button on his remote, the sound of the C4 exploding back-to-back shook the ground violently. Smoke filled the air once the giant safe above them came crashing down to the ground. The explosion caved in more of the roof than Jabari expected, and a few people ended up coming down with the vault. The white dust and smoke fumes were pumping hard, and that was the guy's moment to take advantage. Moving quickly, Teddy moved over to the steel bank and placed another block of Dynamite across the lever. Running back to his corner again

Another explosion ignited, blasting the door across the opposite side of the tunnel. Jabari was the first to move inside the vault. Spotting the clear packaged blocks of money, he started to stuff his duffels with no hesitation. The sewer was foggy, but the crispy hundred-dollar bills were damn sure clear enough to see. It didn't take that long to fill the first bag. Starting on the second one, he struggled to look at the time. Seeing six minutes on the timer, he alerted Teddy and Blow, who were filling their sacks with the loose bills that caved down with the civilians. The bread was plentiful, and their faces were brighter than a child's on Christmas day while snatching up the bundles of cash.

While their minds were occupied on collecting An officer slowly crept up to the giant hole with his flashlight and gun aimed down. His blurry vision made it hard for him to see down inside, but Teddy damn sure wasn't slipping. Raising his Glock 40, he squeezed it twice. Placing one slug to his face, and the other in his chest. The guard flipped directly into the ditch headfirst.

Jabari was stepping out of the safe just as the officer's body hit the ground. Instead of complaining about the stupid decisions his crew was making, he tied his three bags tightly around his shoulders and neck. Before he could speak, his phone began to vibrate.

Whipping it out, he answered without hesitation. "Talk to me?" he barked, still snatching up the extra paper to fill his pockets.

"Jabari, I don't know what the hell y'all knocked down in that bitch, but it sounded like the twin towers fell up here where I'm at. Y'all got a problem, and I mean a bad one. The radios are going off about the officers locking down the entire Nevada. You guys literally got four minutes to get out of that sewer and make it back to the cars or we're all gonna be in jail in the next hour. Get out of the tunnel now," Leo stressed before ending the call.

"We gotta go now!" Jabari shouted, jogging off towards the way they needed to exit. "Let's go! Fuck the rest of that money, nigga. We got four minutes to be outta here and I'm not about to get stuck for neither one of y'all," he said before taking off running down the sewer's concrete sidewalk.

"Nigga, we coming. We coming. This is still like two million down here. We just 'bout to leave all of this?" Blow yelled with a sweaty face. He was still stuffing money on him and started to head behind Teddy and Jabari. Once he realized that they were getting a distance In front of him

The large bags of cash was bouncing heavily across Jabari's back as he ran through the funky shit hole. Making it down to the end of the walkway. He made a left turn that would lead them over to the block where their getaway cars were waiting patiently. The money was beyond heavy, but not enough to make him slow down after the entire plan went accordingly. His energy was on one hundred, and he was sure to control his breathing as he sped down the long trail. Finally spotting the ladder ahead. He reached it and began to climb it faster than he expected. Getting to the top. He pushed the metal plate from its position and raised himself out of the hole. The lights shined slightly in the pathway, and Brandon jumped out of the car as soon as he spotted his brother's presence.

"Bari, are you good?" he asked with worry.

"I'm fine. Pop the trunk and get back in the driver seat now, Brandon." Knocking on Sip's trunk, he got him to release the button and quickly tossed the large bag inside.

Moving back to the sewer, he looked inside and could see Teddy's fat ass struggling with two duffels around his body like that's shit didn't weigh an extra two hundred pounds. Jabari reached his hand down to help him out.

"Just pass the bags up first, idiot," Jabari tried to coach him.

Climbing back down the few steps he made it up, he removed the bags just as Blow was making his way back with the team. One by one, they passed the huge sacks up to Jabari. Every bag that came from out of that tunnel was quickly thrown inside of Sip's trunk. Brandon's car was already filled, and it was guaranteed the best car to divert the police attention clean away from them. After slamming the trunks closed, he reached a hand down and helped Teddy pull himself up out of the filthy hole. The rails inside were drenched with mildew and rat poop. It only took one slip up and a nigga was going back down that bitch for a shit trail, and no more time was needed to be wasted. Once Teddy jumped in the car with Brandon, Jabari helped Blow climb up next and took a deep breath after he was out.

"We did it. The area is beyond hot. Y'all know what to do next. Change cars and we gonna meet up at the location In the desert to head back out to Cali. No stops period," Jabari said with seriousness in his voice.

"Relax Young one. You did it. Be easy and we will see you at the meetup." Blow grinned with excitement before jumping in the passenger seat of Brandon's whip. Watching his little brother crank up, he pulled off and headed in the opposite direction of Sip's car. In order to be successful, they couldn't allow all of the eggs to be in one basket. It was the only reason for splitting up. Once Jabari made the decision to set it up his own way, the plan flowed smoother than Johnson & Johnson's baby oil. Climbing in the front seat of Sip's whip, he wasted no time smashing off. The black Charger he was pushing had enough horsepower to skunk the police by miles. It was easy to slide out of a state with some drugs, but try speaking about seven duffels full of cash that was recently taken from one of the largest casinos in Las Vegas. Nervousness was flushing through his bones, but he was more worried about Brandon than anything. This was the life he wanted to experience, but now this would be the time he would have to open his eyes in order to catch every move that is played into position, or he would only fail like the rest. It was gonna be his process of learning and growing. The same basic rules that Keyno forced him to understand.

"I know you ain't really trying to talk, so I'll just jam to a little music, bro. No rap crap. I can't think with all these damn police riding. Shit got me nervous," Sip mumbled as a police cruiser drove past them slowly. The red light ahead caused Jabari to shake his head in disbelief. Pulling up to the line, the two cops sitting inside the cruiser placed their undivided attention on the nice new model Dodge Charger. Their window slowly began to roll down and the white cop in the passenger seat waved for them to lower theirs also.

"What the fuck does this honkey want, man? I'm not doing shit wrong," Sip uttered a fake smile once it came down far enough for him to speak. "How's it going, officers? Is there a problem?"

"Yeah. That car you're driving. Where did you buy it? Is it a special edition Charger or something? It looks kind of different?" he asked with a raised eyebrow.

"Nahh. It's just a normal ole Charger, sir. I got a little tune-up a while ago, but it's all original." Sip shrugged.

"Mhmm. That's funny. I got the same Charger at home and it's a chip installed in my engine. It's specially made for police, and law enforcement. You can't even purchase it unless you're a licensed officer. They look exactly the same. Every exact detail down to the tires." The officer looked at him with a suspicious grin. "But if you say so. The reason I got your attention is because you have a hundred-dollar bill flapping in the crease of your trunk. Looks like it's fresh from the bank. I know you're probably gonna wanna grab that unless you guys just have money to blow like that." He flashed a crooked smile.

"No sir. I'm Nuwaubian. We keep things in certain spots for our religious beliefs. No big deal." Sip brushed off his nosiness.

"Right. Sure thing. You guys make sure you have a good night. Be careful also. You got men around here robbing the casinos for large amounts of cash. I wouldn't want you to have a run-in with any hooligan who's thinking they got a sweet caper," the officer warned before rolling back up his window.

Laughing off the remark, Sip quickly rolled his window back up and made the first left when the light turned green. His eyes remained in the rearview to make sure they weren't being followed. After cruising down a block or so, he made another right.

"I think those motherfuckers were trying to scope us out. I'm gonna take the short way over to the swap car so we don't have to be on the main street like that," Sip said, thinking they were probably being followed. The hand was always quicker than the eye, and it was instincts that when a man felt a certain way. It was meant to ride with that decision.

Turning down the next backstreet, Sip mashed the gas lightly to place some distance away from the heavily polluted area of cops. The lick was successful and all they had to do now was make it to the safe spot. Moving past an intersecting street, the headlights of a black tinted 2017 Honda shined brightly on the back of his car once it pulled out directly behind them. Jabari glanced in the rearview mirror with a heated expression.

"Who the fuck is these folks blazing their lights on yo whip like that?"

"I don't know. That shit is gay as fuck, man. If they feel like shining bright, they should have made it all the way through high school." Sip laughed before sticking his hand out the window to let them pass in front of him.

Obviously, they took the gesture to slide past because their speed began to slightly pick up. What started as a small acceleration led to the car mashing down heavy on their gas pedal. The car pulled up directly next to the side of them and the M-16 automatic that came out of the window was a sight that Sip didn't expect to see. Jabari was frozen like a deer and before either one of them could blink, shots started ringing out at a rapid pace, shredding the side of the car instantly. The flash from the barrel was glowing like the sun and the sharp hollows were ripping inside the vehicle with a vengeance. One bullet found a home on the side of Sip's head, killing him instantly. Jabari covered his head but still managed to catch a slug to the arm.

"Fuckkkk!" he groaned in pain. The shots were still letting loose, and before he could gain control of the vehicle, it was slamming into a wall at sixty miles per hour. The airbag that released into his face forced his last breath to surface from his lungs before he faded out completely.

The shooter behind the tinted black car skated over quickly to the side of the road when Sip's car collided with the wall. Opening his driver's door, he climbed out with the assault rifle in hand. Loading another full magazine inside the weapon, he aimed and started releasing his second load.

Chris Green

Chapter 11

It had been over two hours since Brandon, Teddy, and Blow arrived at the desert right outside of the Las Vegas city limits. The section was secluded enough to hide anything they had to handle, and it was easy to make a body disappear if it was necessary. Jabari picked the area, and after all the time that had passed, he and Sip still had yet to pull up. The tension was past high. Blow was pacing around with a gun in hand with a furious mug. Not only were these two niggas missing in action, but all the bags of cash they jacked was gone. After noticing it was taking them too long to arrive, he grew suspicious and instantly popped the trunk to check in the stash. Opening the first bag was the fuel to the fire once his eyes roamed around at all the white copy paper wrapped in rubber bands. His hands mashed through the bag noticing that it all was rigged. His head quickly jerked back looking at Teddy, and Brandon recklessly.

"Where the fuck is the dough? Nigga, this is copy paper. What the hell is this?" He threw a handful of the Xerox paper in the air and reached for the next bag. Opening it up, he noticed that the hundred-dollar bills were stacked nearly to the top. He fumbled through most of it to ensure that he wasn't tripping. Zipping back up the duffle, he slid it to the opposite side of the trunk and opened the next. This one was just like the first. Xerox paper filled the inside, no green or blue bills.

"Fuck!" He gritted his teeth. A vein protruded from his neck, and his chest was pumping like he was having a slight panic attack. Teddy moved next to him and looked down at the bag of blank paper.

"What the fuck is going on? I'm not understanding." He scratched his head before picking up a bundle of papers. "This damn sure ain't what we just brought out that motherfucking sewer."

Brandon was lost for words, but it was still all confusing to him. Jabari wouldn't allow anything to stop him from making sure his little brother was secured and safe. He never made a promise that he couldn't keep, and trust was something he would literally lay down and die for. He could tell from the way Blow was twisting up his face that he thought Jabari pulled a slick move. Money was missing. The designated spot for them to meet was still only occupied with their one vehicle, and not one phone call Brandon placed to Jabari's cell phone was answered. Something was more than wrong, but the pieces he needed answers to were missing in action.

Blow turned around, facing them with his lips balled in anger. Without hesitating, he pulled his RugerP98 from his hip and placed a bullet directly in the chamber. "So now I'm guessing you about to say you don't know nothing about this shit, huh?"

Brandon couldn't help but lower his eyes down to the handgun in Blow's hand. He was gripping it tighter than a virgin's pussy and the look of the devil was all in his posture. It was obvious that Blow felt he was involved just from his expression and the frown that formed on Teddy's face let it be known that he was feeling the exact same way. The bubbles in his stomach were starting to form quickly and the worse immediately ran across his mind. Being a part of the robbery wasn't even his option, but from the looks of the way, shit was unfolding. If Jabari didn't happen to show up soon, he was probably gonna be the only one left in the desert decaying for the next two months.

"Blow, I would never take anything from you, period. You're like my big brother too." He swallowed his spit in fear.

"But I'm not yo brother, motherfucka! My bread is the only family I got, but it damn sure ain't sitting here beside me right now. Jabari may be fooling everyone else, but I can smell a snake from ten miles away. How did three bags of Xerox paper get in the trunk of your car and only one bag of cash happened to make it? That means we're missing six bags, my nigga. You were there when he came out that damn sewer. He had three bags around his neck. What the fuck did he do with them?" Blow barked.

Brandon jumped from the sound of his voice, but the gun was more intimidating than anything. "I don't know Blow. He made me get back in the car. I swear man. I wouldn't take shit from you!" he pleaded the truth.

Teddy's hands were on top of his head as he paced back, and forth in a small circle. He knew that Brandon didn't have the mind to even play a dangerous game like that, but Jabari damn sure did. Not only that, but he also knew that Blow was gonna continue to ask until he got fed up. Once his patience runs thin, he was probably gonna snap and murder the young kid in the exact spot he stood. He was beyond mad about the dough also, but allowing him to harm Jabari's little brother would only be innocent blood on his hands when they knew who the blame was supposed to be placed on.

"Listen, Blow. Just calm down and stop waving the gun at him. He's still a kid, bro."

His head rolled around like an owl with a look for blood. "Nigga, I wouldn't give a fuck if he was Jesus' son. My money is missing, and his fuck ass brother got it. How do we know he ain't playing the role with this nigga? We've been waiting in the fucking desert for over three hours and these fools have yet to show. I wouldn't be surprised if he and Sip were on their way to Dubai or some shit right now. He just remixed us, dummy. It's not hard to see," Blow cursed with spittle flying from the side of his mouth.

"I get what the fuck you saying. But now this would be the time to use your head and think about what you're saying. If Jabari was gonna take us off for the money, why in the hell would he place his little brother in jeopardy by leaving him with the same men you taking from? He could've told Brandon to easily climb in the car with him and left us both out here with the sick faces. It's more to the story that we ain't seeing, bruh. That's all I'm saying," Teddy tried to talk some sense into his bird brain.

"Well let's hear it then nigga, cause I could've sworn I've already read this fucking book before when I was on my last bid in the Bay. It was millions in those duffels, Teddy. Millions!" he shouted louder.

"I fucking knowww! I was there too, Blow," Teddy matched his aggression. "If you flip out right now without knowing what the fuck is actually going on, you might do something that you'll regret in the future. First things first. We have to get the hell out of this desert and find out where the hell Jabari is. Once we get that clarified, we will know exactly how to move from there. Trust me, nigga. I want my shit too. Jabari is my friend and all, but if anything, slimy has taken place, then he will have to answer for his actions. But I'll be damn if I catch a life sentence before I can even get a chance to enjoy a piece of this shit. That's what I'm willing to die about right now. I say we get a room at the bottom of Nevada for the night. A small motel until morning where we can clear our thoughts and count the bag we still have in our possession. By sunrise, we will back on the road head in straight for Sacramento."

"We ain't sleeping here period. I don't give a fuck what you say. We driving through the night, and we will make it back quicker than you think. I'm not even giving that boy room to have time with my money. I busted my ass and earned that shit. I want it back or I'll start digging until he pops out of that dirt he hiding under," Blow spat before slamming the trunk closed. "Get in the car. You're staying close until we get this resolved." He motioned Brandon with the pistol to get inside.

Moving with a shaky posture, Brandon shivered lightly and climbed into the backseat. Once he shut the door, Blow looked Teddy in the eyes. "I'm letting you know now. I know this is yo boy, but if we find out he crossed us out that loot, I'm murdering everything that nigga love. Starting with the one in that car," he hissed. The cold-blooded demon was surfacing in his eyes and Teddy couldn't stand to hear the vicious statements any longer.

"Whatever man." He brushed it off with a shrug.

"Yeah, whatever. But do you have a problem with that? Because if you do, there ain't no point of me sticking these keys into that ignition. We can settle it right here cause I'm not allowing nobody to take me down once I start my mission."

Teddy knew what he was insinuating, and he also knew that Blow was serious about killing anyone who stepped in his way. It was a battle that he couldn't win and the screws to his puzzle still needed to be placed together in order for him to make a decision. Instead of hesitating with an answer, he shook his hand firmly. "Just don't move sloppily. Let's try and at least find the money first. After that I don't give a fuck," he replied while shaking his head.

"That's good. Smart man. Let's get the fuck out of here, and go get our shit," Blow agreed and climbed in the driver's seat. Teddy jumped in the front and glanced back at Brandon while he buckled his seat belt. Just from the stale expression on his face, you could tell that he heard every word that was just spoken while he was sitting in the backseat. Breaking his state, Teddy huffed with sorrow, praying to himself that Jabari showed back up before shit went left field. If not, the blood that was about to be shed was a storm that he wasn't going to be able to stop. It was simple. If he flexed them out of the cash and reappeared with no valid excuse, no person or law officer would be able to stop his body from being buried at the bottom of the ocean. That was a promise he made to himself regardless of Blow's moves.

Chapter 12
Blow's Condo
East Side of Sacramento, California

It was around 3:45 when the guys finally arrived back in Cali. The traffic was light, and Blow made sure to keep a buck on the dash the entire drive. His mind was fuming about the foul play of the casino. No one still hadn't received a call, nor a message from Sip, or Jabari. Both of their cells were forwarding everyone straight to voicemail, and the only thing that everyone was trying to know was where the fuck all the cheddar disappeared too. It took Blow to start counting out the duffle bag of money in order to calm down for a second. Teddy sat directly beside him assisting, and Brandon was holding a seat on the living room couch. The count started at least two hours prior, and over eight hundred and forty-grand was accounted for with a little extra to go. It didn't matter about the small change that sat in front of them, because there were still an extra six duffels missing from their possession.

Jabari's eyes were glued to the flat-screen watching the same commercials for the last thirty minutes. The *CNN World News* was finally ending that shit, and all he could think about was how in the fuck the dirty situation between Blow and Jabari was going to end.

After a few ads were shown, the pale CNN newswoman appeared at her oval-shaped desk, nodding with a wide smile. Her blonde hair was sitting gently against her shoulders, and the thin red suit jacket she was wearing allowed the shape of her breast to bulge out with no care, forcing Brandon to double-take.

"Good morning, America. This is *CNN World News* delivering all the stories of the world directly to you. The time is 6:04 A.M., and according to the incidents going on across the globe, we make sure to bring you the most accurate information based on our reports and investigations to ensure that your safety and health issues stay number one with us," she explained, looking down at the papers in front of her. "Leading the cast over to the news story about the Dodge Charger the police found riddled with over thirty-seven bullets in the streets of Las Vegas, Nevada left their police department in shock. According to authorities, the MGM Casino was ambushed last night by a group of robbers who used explosives to remove the vault from its position."

Brandon's heart sped up slightly after hearing her first statement. Grabbing the remote, he turned it up, forcing Teddy and Blow to pause their count and tune in to what all the law enforcement knew.

"I was one of the first on that scene last night for this story and it was obvious that the men who these people are dealing with weren't the average jackers. It took longer than eight hours to get a slight estimate of what was possibly missing, and the range was from anywhere to ten to fifteen million dollars."

Blow cut his eyes over to Teddy with a look of hatred. "Fifteen, nigga," he said through clenched teeth.

Teddy waved his hand lightly trying to calm him and hear what all the reporters claimed to know.

It was a sight that Las Vegas never experienced and surely one that they could never forget at the MGM Casino. Now detectives with the Las Vegas Police Department were called to another scene not too long after the robbery occurred just miles down the road from the casino. The authorities were apparently alerted by a private caller who refused to be identified. The man reported a car that was smashed into the side of a building riddled with bullets. The car was carrying two passengers that were pronounced dead on the scene. The fumes that were leaking from the vehicle caused a small explosion which forced the Dodge Charger to ignite up in flames. The deceased have not been identified by forensics, but the captain of the Las Vegas Police Department made a remark about feeling this incident was definitely related to the robbery of the MGM. After investigators were able to contain the fire, they removed the two bodies and found six burned duffle bags of money that was stashed inside of the trunk. Further research was being pushed to find the whereabouts of the suspects of the homicides, and they should have more information available once the station is alerted with an update.

The tears sitting in Brandon's eyelids felt like two heavy rocks pulling him down to the floor. The sight of Sip's trashed whip was clearly showing that whoever was inside or near that had no chance to make it out alive. Jabari was all he had on his side, and now the world news was actually confirming that his older brother was no longer here. Breaking down with pain written over his face, he screamed loudly into his hands, "Noooo! Please man, this can't be. Please Bari tell me you not gone, bro." He shook lightly as the tears cascaded down his face like a flowing river. "It's not real. It can't be." He rubbed through his hair while looking up into Teddy's eyes.

The pain he was facing at the moment even forced Teddy to drop a tear for the loss of his best friend. The bad feeling, he felt in his gut told him that something else had occurred. Still, not in a million years would he ever think that it would be disturbing news like the shit he just watched. Wiping the wet spots from his cheek, he faced Blow and smirked. "I guess that finally gave you the answers you needed. Shouldn't be any reason to even speak to me about this shit again. Bust my half of the money down later, and I'm getting the fuck out of here after noon. California, this life, the pain. I'm done with it all," he announced before heading back to the guest room.

"So, that's what a nigga do because we lose somebody. You quit like a bitch?" Blow spat with venom.

Teddy forced a small laugh and turned to face him with a harsh frown. "See what I mean. To you, we just lost somebody. But to me and that young one sitting on that couch, we lost a real brother. To me, that's more important than you or any amount of money you could bust a move for. Greediness leads to failure and as long as you're around, this shit will continue to fall until there ain't no one left," Teddy schooled his ass before walking towards the back.

"Well fuck it then nigga. Quit. Money will still be made with or without ya." He shrugged nonchalantly before lighting him a cigar full of exotic.

Brandon was still rocking back and forth on the couch with a destroyed expression. In a matter of seconds, his entire world was crushed. There was no more support. No more great advice when he needed it the most. It was really the last chapter of his life as a child because he would have no choice but to grow into a man if he wanted to survive without Jabari. It didn't matter what amount of money he could possess or how far he could go on his own decisions as a man. Without his other half, he was only a lost soul that was now about to close his heart to everyone who he didn't feel like sincerely cared when his older brother was still breathing. And well, that alone forced the emotional feelings out of his system forever. Wrapping a hand around the diamond necklace, he pulled it close to his lips and placed a kiss on it.

"I promise I won't forget about you, Bari," he mumbled under his breath. The young Brandon who was left alone was now gone. From that day forward, he made a silent promise to himself. No one would ever take him out. And no matter how long it took, he would make sure a bullet was placed through Blow's head at close range. The thought alone gave him chills cause the slimy ass nigga hand tapped his shoulder, offering him the stuffed blunt.

"Aye man, I know how shit may be looking since the world crashing down, but it's the way the game works lil bro," he admitted before Brandon grabbed the blunt, taking a puff.

"Jabari wasn't supposed to go out that way, but what if it was you instead of him. How do you think he would feel right now about his little brother being taken away? It damn sure would be way harder than what you going through because his love for ya was irreplaceable. You was all he gave a fuck about and I bet he would leave it the way it is now in order to make sure you still was able to move around and breathe on this earth, lil nigga," Blow stated, trying to give him the good side to look at it.

Brandon listened closely, but his mind was focused on how to get his vengeance for Jabari's blood being spilled. Talking was the last thing on his mind, especially with the same motherfucker who was prepared to kill him a few hours earlier.

"I understand, but that isn't gonna bring my bruddah back. That's some shit you kick to a smaller child when he doesn't fully grasp what's going on. I'm aware and that will not go unanswered as long as I'm still able to breathe and walk," he promised and leaned back against the couch.

"Respect. Just know that we down for whatever. You still lil bro, so try not to move recklessly unless you're sure that this is what you want. Besides that, we only living in this world. It'll never leave, but we eventually fade away one day. Just try and get some rest. We can put it all together in a few hours after the day starts to roll in." Blow patted his shoulder and headed for the room.

Brandon's mind was so polluted that the weed only forced him to think about more violence. The dizzy aura spinning around in his brain caused him to lean back to try and relax. Thoughts were moving a million miles a minute that it forced him to slowly drift off into a light snooze.

Chris Green

Chapter 13
Three Hours Later

"Motherfuckerrr!" Blow shouted, slamming the empty duffle bag against the glass table. The loud thud caused Brandon to jump out of his sleep looking confused.

"What's going on?" he asked while rubbing his eyes and standing to his feet.

Both his hands were covering his face tightly, as he mumbled something in a low tone. Exhaling, he cut his eyes over to Brandon. "How long were you sleep, nigga?"

"I don't know. I guess until you just woke me with all that loud ass noise. Why?"

"Because. The fucking money is gone, and Teddy is nowhere to be found!" he snapped with his arms held out in disbelief.

"What? Why would he do that? Did you try and call him? Maybe he was just securing the bag to ensure y'all didn't take another loss."

Blow cleared his throat and slid the small fake ass note Teddy left across the table. His eyes fell on the scribbled words reading them carefully. "You feel untouchable. I feel like this was owed to me. That makes two different reasonings, so it's no reason for me to even bargain with splitting shit. Catch me when you can."

Brandon raised his head with a surprised face. "This nigga just took the whole million and didn't leave our shit?"

"No duh. Clearly, it's gone 'cause it damn sho ain't sitting where I left it," he replied in a sarcastic tone. Moving over to the tall wooden entertainment center. Blow reached behind it and removed an all-black HP14 assault rifle. The clip that was hanging from the bottom was shaped like a banana and a small red beam was mounted directly on the side just a few inches away from the trigger loop. Pulling the hammer back a tad to check the barrel, he racked it back, placing one in the head.

"I'm about to go hunt this nigga down until I find it. I don't give a fuck where his ass is laying low at. Any friends, family, I'm killing their ass one by one until every fucking coin is returned. You know more than I do, and your money is tied up in this shit too. Are you riding or what?" Blow slid the pistol from his waistline holding it out for him to grab.

Looking at it for a slight second, Brandon paused. Gripping it by the handle, he slid it on his waistline and covered the handle with his shirt. "Yeah, I'm riding. I ain't got a choice. That money is all I got to my name, man." He frowned.

"Good choice. I'm letting you know that if we catch his ass, he's dead. We can split that shit down the middle after that and both of us walk away happy," Blow lied knowing that he would comply.

"I said I'm down. Why we still sitting here?"

Giving him a solid nod, they both turned and headed out of the front door. Teddy was doing more than just taking them off for the money, he was letting it be known that getting anything back from his possession was officially out of the question. The city of Sacramento was large, and when people roamed through different parts of Cali, it could be nearly impossible to track someone down. Brandon knew that Teddy was beyond serious, but now that ugly situation he almost got caught up in earlier in Nevada was about to flip back against his ass a hundred times harder. Or so they thought.

* * *

Jabari's Funeral
Six Days Later

Even though the rain was drizzling down smoothly against Brandon's skin, his tears could be seen pouring down harder. Placing the rose on top of his brother's closed casket, he touched the top of his framed picture. So many people were in attendance for Jabari's burial. Old school teachers and principals, nearly every girl he ever spoke to in class or throughout the entire South Hagginwood. Even a few of the original OG's out the hood tucked their flag out of respect for the young one who didn't bend or fold for anyone. He was like the superhero for the youths around Sacramento. More than just encouragement to do better in school, but even within the neighborhood. It was a solid reason why every soul was in attendance that day. Nearly all of the guests were shedding a few sobs and hugs while mourning their loss, but Brandon was the one that really needed the most support at the time. It had been over fifteen minutes and his legs were glued in the same spot as if the casket was about to leave his sight at that exact moment. The hurt was unbearable, but he managed to face his loved ones and grab the microphone from the small podium. Clearing his throat, he gazed around at the large crowd nervously.

"I'm not quite sure what to say at the moment, so I'll just express the way I see things through my vision about my brother." He paused once more. "Jabari was the one that everybody could call a leader. This was the one, and only role model for me as a child while growing up in these wild streets of Sacramento. I watched him grow not only mentally and physically, but spiritually as well. His words brightened with every day that passed, and that glow above his head started to shine harder once he let go of faulting himself about stuff that was out of his control. He was always trying to save the world and never even thought to make sure it was all good with himself. It's the reason I respect my brother more than any man that I've ever met in my life."

Detective Shannon sat at the second to last row soaking in the speech Brandon was pouring from his heart. Her black shades made it easier for her to blend in and even after witnessing all the funeral process, she still couldn't believe that he was actually gone. Her case was placed on pause and the investigation of all his associates was the way she needed to dig deeper. A feeling in her gut said that it was more to the tragedy and by any means necessary, Shannon was going to squeeze those information seeds out of someone.

"I'm proud to say that even though I have to experience this dark pain, for now, I'm glad that my brother can be at peace and finally get the love and support that he deserves. He will always be missed but never forgotten. That's a promise that I can and will keep for eternity. Jabari, we love you. Until the end of time when we meet again twin," Brandon said before locking eyes on the Grey Mazda that was sitting in the street. The window was rolled down showing enough of his face to make his entire thought process go out of the window.

"Son of a bitch," he whispered, dropping the mic and moving swiftly through the aisle of chairs.

Blow caught his movements and followed his eyes to the center of the one-way street. His sight tried to lock in closer on the person behind the wheel and for a second, he could've sworn that Teddy was behind the driver's seat. As he took a step forward, the window began to slide back up and the car started to drive swiftly away from the scene before anything could get out of hand.

Just as Brandon reached the edge of the curb, Detective Shannon Kegg called out his name to snag his attention. Turning around to face her, his frown sent a slight chill up her spine. It was nearly like looking at Jabari in a younger form.

"Who are you?" he checked her immediately.

"Uh, my name is Detective Shannon Kegg with the Sacramento Police Department. It's nice to meet you." She held her hand out for him to shake.

Cutting his eyes at her dangling hand, he left it in thin air and humbled himself. "What do you want, and is there any reason you're at my brother's funeral?"

"I'm actually a close friend, and I wanted to show my condolences. Jabari and I were set to meet up a few weeks ago before this occurred and build on what his plans were for the small business that he wanted to invest in. I was establishing things piece by piece and that's when I got the terrible news." She removed her glasses out of respect.

"Yeah. It's crazy, but it's okay. I'm still trying to cope and mingle around to see what all he had in effect to be processed. I'm sure if you two were close like you say, it should be documented already and I can finish the process right up for you," Brandon assured with a straight face. "How come I never met you?" He titled his head slightly to the side.

"Uhh, well, I'm sure that it was bound to come soon, but Jabari only got a chance to meet with me a few times before I really found out who you were," she remixed her story quickly to keep his mind in think mode.

"I see." Brandon nodded. "Well Ms. Kegg, I'm sure that I can research you guys' paperwork to ensure all still goes well. If you need to, I can give you a lift to his home where we can pull up the documents from his laptop."

Before she could answer, Blow pulled up and interrupted their conversation as if she wasn't visible. "Nigga, did you just see what I saw or am I tweaking?"

Holding up a finger to silence him, Brandon cleared his throat to alert him about Shannon. "Uh yeah. I did and I'm trying to finish this situation with Detective Shannon here. If you don't mind, I just need a second."

Blow's heart skipped a beat, and the swine could be smelled coming straight from the bitch's body. She was definitely a cop. "Sure thing."

"Uh, are you a close friend of the family also?" She turned her attention to Blow.

"Nah, I'm just security," he lied before taking a few steps back so they could continue.

Brandon held his hand out with a small smile before she could ask anything else. "I don't mean to be pushy, Detective, but I still have a lot of family to attend to and my time is short. If you have a card, I'll be sure to call when I get the slightest chance."

She smiled, removing one from her purse. "Please do."

As she spent on her heels to leave, a nasty thought about setting her ass up crossed his brain. Jabari was a nice individual. A smart one at that, but he was never too familiar with cops, and that's where Detective Shannon flushed her entire story. She was now added to the watch list in Brandon's eyes.

Blow wasted no time pulling back up once his eyes spotted her climbing inside of an unmarked Denali. "Nigga, why is a cop at this man's funeral? What did she say?" he asked nervously.

"Obviously she's snooping. Can't be nothing major if no one is leaving in handcuffs. I'll stay on it just to be sure. But yes, that was Teddy posted in the Mazda watching us. He knew that nothing would be able to pop off here like that. We gotta find him," Brandon sighed.

"You don't say. It's been a week. I searched top and bottom for this bitch. He can't hide forever and his sister ain't staying out in Old Sacramento no more."

Brandon's attention moved over to Victoria who slowly approached him through the small field of grass. Her beautiful black hair was hanging down her back. She was dressed nicely in her Valentino dress and heels matched the black purse that rested under her arms.

"Brandon, I know that this is a hard time for us all right now, but I really need to speak with you about something very important when you get the chance." Her eyes glowed with sadness and he could tell that Jabari's death was eating her apart.

"Are you okay? I'm available now for you." He placed a hand on her shoulder.

Cutting her eyes over to Blow, she paused and stumbled over her next sentence. "This isn't the right place. I need to speak with you in private, not over the phone. Face to face," Victoria pleaded through her eyes as if she was trying to warn him.

Brandon could feel her energy but didn't let it show. Instead, he played it smooth to not raise any suspicion. "Okay. I'll come over as soon as I get the chance," he guaranteed.

Victoria quickly nodded and slid from his presence.

"Who the fuck is that?" Blow asked with a hint of anger.

"It's Jabari's girl," Brandon stated, not wanting to explain too much.

"That's Victoria, How come she ain't been around, but fin time to make it to bro's funeral?"

"Not sure. They kept their relationship personal, and she barely came over unless he wanted her to." He shrugged.

"She damn sho gave me a nasty look when you asked her to talk like she didn't want to say shit in front of me or sum." Blow frowned.

"Nah, man. She just fucked up bout bro," Brandon said to end the guessing game. He didn't know what Victoria had to say, but it wasn't about to be spoken on in front of him for damn sho. "Look, man. I'm about to finish greeting the rest of these people, and I'll link up with you after," he said before dispersing back over to the burial site.

"Yeah, you do that." Blow nodded, sensing his vibe change. Turning around to face the guest. His eyes happened to find Victoria's. Fear was instilled in her expression, and it clarified more than enough for him. That bitch had something to say, and he was damn sure about to find out. Flashing a half-smile, he lightly waved at her before turning to leave the cemetery.

Chapter 14
Cynthia's Bakery
8:16 A.M.

The sky was shining bright and the cool breeze from Cynthia's air conditioner was finally back working properly. She and Victoria moved around the shop preparing the fresh coffee and bagels before the customers arrived. It was always natural to receive a small load on the weekdays when the college kids needed a place to grab a bite for breakfast, and she didn't want to miss any of the income that could help her and Victoria build their own way out of California. Things were getting back on track, but for the past few days, she could sense that Victoria was not pleased anymore. Especially after she explained the tragedy with Jabari. It was hurtful to see her in so much pain after waiting so long to find her happiness. Cynthia knew that it was all a part of God's creation, but adhering and accepting that was just so hard to do.

As Victoria sprayed some cleaner around the tables to wash them off, her peripheral spotted the seven black Mercedes Benz Sedans pulling in front of their store back-to-back. The tints were covering the occupant's identity, and they sat for at least thirty seconds before the first car door opened. A tall Italian man with a brown fedora hat stepped smoothly out the driver's side and dusted off his black trench coat. He observed the scenery both ways before tapping on the hood, alerting the rest that it was clear to move. The following car doors opened at once, and numerous Italians began to pour from each side until the Boss of Bosses risen from the last car.

Victoria gasped seeing his face, and the hairs on her neck stood out like an arrow. The men moved smoothly towards the entrance until the bell signaled that someone was entering. Cynthia was pulling a fresh batch of muffins from the oven and happened to turn around. When she looked up at the men standing in her bakery, The pan crashed to the floor.

"Frankie?" She shuddered with chills just from mumbling his name. Victoria remained in the corner frozen like a piece of snow.

Eleven of the men made their way over to a section and took a seat while one walked up to the counter. "Cynthia, it's great to see you. How about a round of bagels and coffee for the guys? Frankie would like to have a word with you." Vinnie smiled before leaning in to place a kiss on her cheek.

"Sure thing, Vinnie." Her hands trembled slightly from the surprise visit. Without hesitation, she grabbed a large platter, placing twelve coffee mugs on top. Filling them all to the rim, she gathered a bundle of bagels and cheese adding it to the side. Victoria finally slid over to the counter to give her mother some assistance and her eyes were blinking faster than a cheetah.

"What is he doing here?" she whispered while grabbing a few napkins and plastic spoons.

"I don't know baby, but it's damn sure nothing good." Cynthia flashed a fake smile before sliding a large butcher knife into her giant apron.

Taking the lead, Cynthia picked up the coffee tray and headed straight over. Her expression stated that all was good, but her posture was showing different. All eyes were on her until she reached the table. Sitting the coffee and bagels down, she stood up straight and smirked.

"If it isn't Mr. Omerta himself. What do I owe for this visit, Frankie?" She placed a hand on her hip.

Frankie smiled and reached for a cup of coffee. Taking a small sip, he placed it gently back down the table. "How have you been Cynthia? It's been a very long time."

"Living. Not much left to do since I left Italy," she replied dryly.

Frankie tilted his head with a nod. He was the real boss of the Mafia. The top Don is what they would call him back home. He was powerful through the underworld business and had his hands in over thirty businesses across America. He was dangerous and mostly known for the ruthless Italians who moved with him every second of the day. Cynthia's husband, Benny the Bull, was his Capo before he was found with two slugs in the back of his head on their sixteenth anniversary. He always claimed that he never played a part in his death, but the Dons who truly respected her power and husband continued to mention Frankie's name when the subject was brought up. Every last one of those men was executed until they finally made him the top Don of the Italian Mafia.

"Cynthia, I've always respected you to the fullest. I mean you're Benny's wife and that was my brother. It was a duty to protect and provide for you after he passed, and I never was allowed that chance. I hope that you know nothing has changed about that promise. You can come home and run your spot in this family as you did from the start. I mean you have Victoria down here living as a table girl. That's not the life Benny wanted for her."

"Benny's gone Frankie, and I don't need anything from you. This is my home."

Frankie's twin son, Mickey, broke out with a sinister laugh as if her statement tickled him. He was silenced when his father snapped a finger. "You have to forgive him, Cyn. He's not used to hearing Italians speak so reckless about home in these American's territory."

Standing to his feet, Frankie walked over to her until they stood face to face. "Unfortunately, I have a problem and I'm here to fix it. I've heard from a few birdies that you may know where Vinnie's daughter is? Apparently, she's been violating the family code with this black guy who just so happened to rob my fucking casino for fifteen million dollars. You wouldn't have happened to hear anything about that, would you?" Frankie folded his arms calmly.

Cynthia's face screwed up. "No, Frankie. Why would I know about something like that? I haven't seen Vinnie's daughter in months besides the few times she's come through the shop to eat after school."

"I believe you. I honestly do, but that doesn't mean that I can say that same for her." He tilted his head looking past her at Victoria. "What do you say, sweetie? You mind if we sit down for a second to figure this out?"

Cynthia looked back at her with a raised brow. "Victoria, what's going on? Have you heard anything about this?"

She exhaled while twiddling with her fingers nervously before walking over to them.

* * *

Ben Ali Neighborhood
Leo's House

Veronica rotated her hips in a circular motion on top of Leo enjoying her second session for the morning. His hands gripped her bottom as she grinded gently on his manhood. Their lips locked sharing a kiss while he laid down his sex game properly. As she stared into his eyes, their foreheads touched, and he finally released himself inside of her. After a few more strokes, their hard breathing and smooches were all they had enough energy to do.

Rolling off of him, Veronica's heart nearly jumped out of her chest staring at her father and his henchmen standing in Leo's bedroom doorway. "Oh my God daddy! I can explain!" She jumped into the corner using the sheet to cover her naked body.

"What the fuck? How did y'all motherfuckers get in my house?" Leo shouted, trying to stand to his feet.

Frankie's son, Mickey, pulled his chrome 9mm from his shoulder holster crashing it across his nose and breaking that shit instantly.

"Goddamnittt! What's going on man?" he cried as blood started to rush from his face.

Vinnie was so distraught from the sight he was seeing that he couldn't even speak. He was sure that if Frankie would of came inside his entire respect for their family would have been deleted from the Italian bloodline completely. Walking over to her, Vinnie grabbed her by the hair, snatching Veronica to her feet. His lips were curled in anger and his right fist was balled so tight that he nearly broke a finger.

"Are you stupid or have you lost your fucking mind? You've broken our family code for this black piece of shit! Is this the guy that robbed Frankie's business? Is it?" he screamed before pushing her towards a few of the other Dons that stood guard. "Get her the fuck out of here."

Vinnie looked down at Leo holding his face and squatted down next to him. "Hey kid, I want one answer only. And if I hear anything different, I'll make you take a trip to hell before you could remember how good that sex was. The casino. You took something that didn't belong to you. Where is it?" Vinnie asked through clenched teeth.

"I don't know what you're talking about man," Leo panted, looking down at the floor.

Vinnie rubbed the bridge of his nose and pulled a picture of Leo out the night he was walking through the MGM Casino and shoved it in his face. "I guess you don't know Leon Jackson either, huh motherfucker. Take him up top and show him the view. Will ya, Mickey?" he ordered before leaving out the bedroom door.

One henchman helped Mickey pick Leo up to his feet and headed straight for the patio's porch upstairs. When Vinnie stepped out on the front porch, He walked down the steps towards the line of Mercedes Benz that blocked off the small street. Veronica was wrapped in a sheet standing next to Vinnie's top shooter. Walking over to Frankie's car first, he watched the window roll down just enough to see his eyes. "Did you find my money?"

"Not yet Frankie, but I'm sure she knows. I found the kid and he's denying it just like you said," Vinnie confirmed.

Frankie pulled on his cigar and blew a cloud of smoke up into his face. "Then why did you walk over to my car, Vinnie?" he stated before rolling his window back closed.

Feeling a bubble gut in his stomach, he tightened his trench and headed over for his daughter. Pointing a finger in her face, he snarled, "You're gonna tell me where that money is, and everybody involved. I promise if you don't, you'll never be able to speak about it again."

Mickey and the henchmen who were left with Leo stepped out on the small balcony just as the last few words left from Vinnie's lips. A thick brown rope was now tied around his neck. His hands and feet were bound in cuffs. You could clearly see that they beat him to a pulp before allowing his face to hit the sun. His naked body was barely able to stand, and Mickey's evil smile stated what was about to happen next.

Vinnie turned around to face them and nodded in approval. Grabbing Veronica's chin, he forced his daughter to look up at the porch. "This is what happens to a fucking mooly that disrespect this family."

Placing Leo on the edge of the rail, Mickey tied it to the guard post and kicked him with a hard foot to the back. His body slung forward, and Veronica's eyes closed after his neck snapped smoother than a chicken. He dangled from the two-story home with his eyes bulging with pain. The terror was just beginning. Before Vinnie allowed the cause of the Mafia falling to its demise, he was gonna wake Sacramento up with a new death toll. Whatever Frankie wanted until he received every coin back in his possession.

Chris Green

Chapter 15

Pulling her silver four-door Lexus into her sister's driveway, Shannon shut off her engine and stepped out of the car. Remembering to slide over and grab the files she stashed regarding her past investigations, she stopped by before heading to the precinct. Using the key that she was given, Shannon walked inside and locked the door behind her. The first thought was to head for the computer office down in the basement until she heard Sarah's voice. She was speaking to someone. That was awkward being that she shared a home with no one, and around this early morning she would be out of the house and heading for work. Rerouting her movements, Shannon walked lightly up the stairs and surely her sister's voice began to rise.

"Why didn't you just take me with you? People are asking too many questions, and I don't know what to do anymore. I never wanted this life, but you showed me." Sarah moved around her room, expressing herself to the unknown caller.

Shannon's antennas began to rise from her statement, so she placed her ear lightly to the bedroom door.

"No, I don't ever want to see a bank again!" Sarah huffed with exhaustion.

That word alone forced her to grab the doorknob and enter.

Sarah's head jerked around looking Shannon in the face and quickly hung up the phone. "Oh my God, Shannon! What are you doing here? What the hell are you just barging into my room for?" She stood up, placing the phone behind her back.

"Who were you talking to?"

"No one, just a friend." Her vision lowered showing that she was obviously lying.

"You mind if I see?" Shannon held out her hand.

"What? No Shannon. I'm not a child. You can't check me, and this is my home," she stressed, trying to stand up for herself.

Walking over to Sarah, she reached behind her, snatching the touchscreen with ease.

"What the fuck are you doing? It's my business, Shannon. I fucking hate you!"

"I know." She ignored her while swiping to the call log. The last number was a private call, so was the recent fifteen that was days before. "So, you're dealing with a friend who's calling you private?"

Sarah tapped her foot angrily, but didn't respond.

"Okay." Shannon shrugged. Pulling the sim chip from her phone, she tossed it back on the bed and walked out.

"You're never gonna win, Shannon. You always lose because you're so miserable. Just like dad. Stay away from me and be sure to leave the key on your way out!" she screamed before slamming her bedroom door.

Ignoring her slurs and rage, Shannon snatched her files from the basement and made her way back outside to the car. Tossing it all on the backseat. Her phone vibrated. It was a call from the department. "This is Detective Shannon Kegg."

"Shannon, we need you at the office immediately!" a voice spoke through the line.

"Johnson..." She paused. "Is everything okay?"

"Not this time, Shannon. It's a nightmare down here. Its Pakori," he informed.

The bad feeling in her gut said that it wasn't nice from the sound of his voice. Jumping into her driver's seat, she started the engine. "I'm on the way." Her phone was tossed in the passenger seat before swerving recklessly out of the parking lot.

Sarah watched from her upstairs window and grabbed her spare cell once Shannon's car was no longer in sight. Before she could even pray about receiving a call. The line began to ring.

"Hello?" she fumbled to answer quickly.

"Yeah."

"I think she knows."

* * *

Sacramento Police Department
Federal Crime Scene

As Shannon made it down to the street of her department, she could barely make it through from all the ambulances and authorities that surrounded the area. Federal agents, duty officers, and SWAT members patrolled around the four intersecting blocks, and the helicopter was floating in a circle to ensure no movement was allowed until their suspects were caught.

Climbing out of her car, Shannon rushed towards the crime scene tape and stepped under it. Detective Brunner Johnson was engaging in a conversation when she stepped up to him. The sight of Captain Pakori's cruiser was hideous. Blood was splattered on the side of the windows. A large bullet hole was lodged through the middle of the driver's window, but the worse part was the sight of his decapitated head chilling on top of the hood. It was battered and bruised viciously. Shannon immediately turned her head from the scene before she puked everywhere. Placing a hand on her forehead, she took a deep breath and Detective Johnson came to quickly console her.

"I didn't want you to see this, but we had no choice. They're placing you in charge of the department, and your father has been here for the last hour. Seven people have already lost their jobs and I am not trying to be next," he admitted.

Shannon held up a finger, blowing a fresh breath of air, trying to control the wave of nausea. "What the fuck is going on here? My boss' head is sitting on the hood of a police car in front of the station. How in the hell does something like that occur when this building is open 24/7?"

"That's what we're trying to figure out now. The cameras are being reviewed, and we have a search team at his house looking for his daughter, and wife. They're nowhere to be found, and his house was completely destroyed.

Turning back around, she glanced at Pakori once more. It was sad to see the man who showed her so much about the enforcement suffered a horrible death as the one he did, but it also meant that foul play was surely in the mixture. "Where's my father?" she asked, snapping a few pictures of the crime scene.

"He's over by SWAT van speaking with the forensics doctor. He's pissed and he wants answers." Johnson shrugged before walking off to assist his other duty officers.

Shannon moved through the large parking lot until she locked in on her father ordering people to do their job correctly. His hand was waving around angrily, and it was definitely gonna be a hard day when he had to fly all the way from D.C to help out with a catastrophe like the one they had on their hands.

Shannon closed the distance between them and tapped on his shoulder. "Why didn't you tell me that you were here? Don't you think it should be known if my department has an emergency that I should be alerted, daddy?" She gave him a look as if he was being checked.

Folding his arms, his eyes squinted low in anger. "Shannon, this is your department. Don't you think that someone should have alerted you about this before me? Why in the hell do I have to get woken up at three in the morning and have to leave the president's side for a station you're supposed to be a leader in?" he turned the question back against her.

Before she could answer, his phone buzzed loudly. Removing it from his vest pocket, he answered without checking the number. "This is Kegg."

"And this is Frankie, I guess you've arrived in Cali and have seen my work? We need to speak Patrick and I don't mean tomorrow," he threatened him indirectly.

The sound of his old associate's voice made him cringe. Just the scenery alone let him know that this was his work. Or maybe even the two demons he raised as sons, Mickey and Mikey. Knowing that he was dealing with a powerful force, he chose his words carefully. Holding up a hand for his daughter to be silent, he stepped a few feet away and spoke into the receiver, "What the hell have you done, Frankie?"

"It's not what I've done, Patrick. It's what your precious daughter's city has done to me," he replied calmly.

Shannon looked over at him with a confused face wondering why he had to distance himself for a call dealing with law enforcement business. Family was never off-limits to knowing what was taking place and at that moment he was switching on his own statements which were something Patrick didn't do.

"I don't know what the fuck you're talking about, Frankie. My daughter has no ties with you and don't you ever fix your mouth to make it that way. It's been years Frankie. We've settled our disputes," Patrick tried to reason with him.

"Truth. I respect you, Patrick, but it seems that things have changed. I'm sure you watch the news, correct? I mean, for Christ's sake, most of the shit that happens on this planet falls right on your desk. My casino was robbed for fifteen million dollars. And the dirty thieves happened to run back to your daughter's city. I'm sure

Pakori was gonna be a hard ass, so I gave him the blessings of having my presence first. I need that back Patrick or Sacramento will never be able to sleep again. I'll sleep peacefully of course, but Mickey and Mikey will keep these streets awake like breakfast from granny on a Sunday morning. Is that understood, or should I continue my search on my own?" he questioned.

"Give me a few days to find out what's going on Frankie. I'll handle it. That's my word, but I can't do anything if you're raising the death rate," Patrick bargained.

"Ummm, I think I'll allow you to do that, *but* I'm still gonna have a little fun. Just a little, Patrick." Frankie chuckled before leaving him with the main screen on his phone.

Placing the cell back in his pocket, he rubbed his chin and headed back over to Shannon. "I need you to find out what's going on with this problem and I mean immediately. This is bigger than what you think Shannon. Stay off the radar and don't discuss anything with any lower ranks. I'm receiving word about a backlash of the MGM Casino robbery. Pakori has some dirty gloves hidden and we need to find them before this spirals out of control. I'm gonna stick around for a few days, and call you when I figure out more," Patrick ordered and walked off before she could even ask a question.

"Wait, Daddy... What does a casino have to do...Dad!" she called out to him as he kept walking through the thick crowd.

His entire mood had changed, and it was definitely something he wasn't telling her. The marines and forces gave her the gift to spot it out instantly. Getting Detective Johnson's attention, she waved him over.

"Yes ma'am?" He stood at attention while waiting for her command.

"I need you to dig in the system for an old address. The father of Jabari Salters."

"Right away ma'am," he said before heading into the department building.

There was only one person she knew that can pull off a smooth criminal mission like the MGM Casino, and he was laying inside of a coffin. The next in line was a sixteen-year-old that she knew had something to hide. If it was deep enough where Captain Pakori lost his life and her father was acting awkwardly, there was a puzzle still missing a few pieces and she was gonna make sure she found Brandon before it found him.

Chris Green

Chapter 16
Vinnie's Beach House
Long Beach, California

Hearing a door open and close loudly, Veronica jumped in the chair that she was bound to. A pillowcase was over her head blocking her vision from being able to see. After a small moment of silence, the thin fabric was snatched from her head, blinding her for a slight second. The smell of fresh water was lingering through the back-porch window. A small fresh banquet of breakfast food was sitting on top of the table waiting to be eaten. Veronica looked down at the warm cup of tea in front of her and back up at Vinnie who sat on the opposite side of the table. His napkin was tucked neatly into his collar shirt and he was calmly enjoying a fresh single pancake with a side of grapes. His eyes rose, locking in on her shaky expression.

"Do you want something to eat or drink?" he asked humbly.

The bodyguard standing next to her was looking down into her soul like a hawk and it damn sure wasn't a lustful gaze. More like a thirst for blood. Instead of replying verbally, she shook her head.

"Okay." Vinnie shrugged, and sat his fork down. The napkin in his shirt was used to quickly wipe his mouth before he sat back to observe her. "Veronica, I don't think you realize what you have just done to me. Not only did you embarrass me as a father, but you've put our lives in jeopardy with the same people I call family. The blueprints of Frankie's casino was taken and you were in charge of that department. Your boyfriend was caught snooping on the night of the hit, and it's all falling back to you, honey. I need you to tell me who has that money."

Veronica's hands trembled knowing she was caught with her palms in a cookie jar. Fear for the consequences was scarier as she watched her father speak calmly to her. "I'm s—sorryyy," she stuttered. "I didn't mean to hurt you, daddy." Her eyes pleaded for his forgiveness.

Vinnie sat up in his chair with a blank expression. "Honey, fifteen million dollars has been taken from the man that I work for. I'm afraid that sorry can't cut it. I need names and places to go, Veronica. Please baby. I can't help what happens after you've shown such disloyalty. Who has the money?"

Thinking of who to give up, the first name that came to mind spilled from between her lips, "Blow...His name is Blow." She nodded with assurance.

"Blow? What does this guy look like? Where does he live? I need more baby?"

"That's all I know," she lied, feeling that Jabari's associates would surely hunt her down about Leo being murdered. Italians vendetta with the blacks would leave no excuse for them to spare her soul once she was caught. She was truly ready to take her chances with her father knowing how much she meant to her mother. "It's all I know. That's it, daddy. I swear." Her face was betraying the fake innocence she poured out.

Rubbing his temples, Vinnie sighed. "Okay, darling. I'll give you a few more hours to think this over and we can go from there. I'm warning you, Veronica. I can't protect you, honey. It's either me or you, and I refuse to make a will for a mistake that you made," he stated before standing up.

"Daddy, I-" her words were cut short from the pillowcase sliding back over her face.

Vinnie made his way to the front of his home preparing to head back up to Sacramento. Whoever Blow had a rude awakening coming and Vinnie "Two Times" was gonna be the one presenting it personally. Using his phone, he dialed Frankie's cell.

After two rings, he answered. "Vinnie?"

"I found the names and I'm on the way. If I don't find him after the first hour of my arrival, she's gonna be dismissed, and I'll handle the business personally."

"Family first Vinnie. Don't make me hate you. I love you, but could also hate you," he said with a cold tone.

"I won't Frankie. That's a promise of the la familia." He ended the call. Huffing, he watched as his guard placed Veronica in the backseat of a Tahoe truck. Vinnie slid on a pair of fresh black leather gloves and climbed into the front seat of his black Lincoln Navigator. It was a vehicle that he hated to bring out of retirement, but the situation at hand left no choice. Murder was needed, and people were about to see why they called him the nightmare of Two Times. Before you thought your life was gone, he would spare you and take it again. The omerta team was coming back to town, and nothing would be able to stop their path of destruction. Not even the all-merciful.

Chris Green

Chapter 17
Sports Bar and Grill
South Hagginwood
9:39 P.M.

After driving around collecting information about this mystery bitch of Jabari's. Blow swerved his whip over in the parking lot of the local bar for a quick drink. His mind was running in overload about the shitty week he suffered though that he was willing to kill any motherfucker who gave him a sideways look. It had been solid at first, but now shit was smelling funny. So much money had been snatched from his possession that he cursed himself for not placing a bullet through every last one of the young niggas who slept around him. News about Leo being killed had him knowing that some strange shit was surfacing around the city fa sho.

Climbing out his whip, he lit a Newport and looked up into the night sky. A helicopter was floating above him moving towards the downtown area. It was on fire in Sacramento, but shit needed to stay balanced in order to keep a radar from his face until all business was taken care of.

Walking in the large sports grill, Blow made his way up to the middle bar and took a seat at the stool in front of him. The flat-screen behind the bartender was airing the *World News*, and the one next to it was showing a heated football game between the Green Bay Packers and the Kansas City Chiefs. The nice slim woman dressed in black walked over to him with a bright smile, wiping her hands.

"How are you today, handsome? Can I get you anything?"

"Just a shot of Henny and a Heineken beer. Keep the change," he grumbled, sliding a fifty-dollar bill across the table.

"Sure thing. Coming right up." She grabbed the bill before walking to the sidebar for a fresh bottle.

The place was over packed, and the noise level was on a hundred from the rival football game. Blow didn't give a damn about that and the cigarette in his hand was starting to give him a slight headache. Tossing it to the side, his eyes happened to look up at the television that was showing the news. The title 'Las Vegas Murder' was crossing the small of the screen causing him to tune in harder. Grabbing the small remote in front of him, he turned up the volume to the max in order to hear the reporter.

"In other news, we have more information about the mystery car that was shot up and smashed into the side of a Las Vegas building almost two weeks ago. The authorities made a terrible mistake in the report and had to clarify that there was only one body of a man found inside of the burning vehicle. Apparently, the investigator made an error with the information upon it being given to the news channel and has been placed under investigation when the law enforcement discovered that he was paid to lie about the crime scene. Las Vegas Captain Logan of the department has made a statement about the sloppy detectives who allowed something so serious to happen that numerous officers had been placed on paid leave until the investigation has ended. Most of the men are facing jail time for false information and tampering with federal evidence. Those charges alone could have them facing up to fifteen years in prison, including fees that round off to five hundred thousand dollars. More about this mysterious case will be coming soon and that's all we have for now. This is reporter, Kelly Fisher, with the coverage for the *CNN World News*. Have a good day."

Blow's entire anger radar began to rise faster than a burning thermometer. He was so busy staring at the television that he never noticed the bartender sit his drinks down in front of him. Snapping out of the bloodthirst trance, the first thing that came to his mind was Victoria's sheisty ass face at the cemetery. Brandon was most definitely gonna have to answer a few questions personally face to face. This would be the time where he either spilled the beans or lost his life where he stood.

Grabbing the shot of Hennessey, he downed it quickly and followed suit with the beer. Standing to leave, he turned to his right and froze in shock. His eyes had to be playing tricks on him because this nigga was sloppy drunk sitting twenty feet away at a table with a slut. A black fitted cap was pulled down over his head and he was leaning on the hoe like that pitcher of beer and shots had him drunk as fuck. You could tell the bitch was a skeezer because she pushed his ass back over every time he slumped over.

Blow was sure to hold his head low but kept an eye on him closely. He watched Teddy stand to his feet and pulled up his crispy skinny Zara jeans. He could tell the nigga had been spending some dough from the Christian Louie's he had strapped on his feet. The knots in his jeans said that something was on him and Blow was not about to let him slide away again. The blessing came perfectly because Teddy said something to his little date and headed for the men's bathroom stumbling hard as shit. It gave Blow the perfect opportunity to slide away from the bar and follow him.

By the time Blow reached the section of bathrooms, the small hallway was empty, and Teddy had already made his way inside. He pulled a Glock 23 pistol from his hip, holding it out in front of him before walking smoothly inside.

The clean white room brightened when he stepped through the door, and Teddy stood at a piss stall with his head buried against the wall. His pants were down to his thighs and his bitch ass could barely stand up to urinate properly. Blow crept up behind him slithering like a snake in the grass. His pupils were wide, and Teddy lifted his head at the right time. The reflection of Blow could be seen in the porcelain toilet reflection. That shit sobered his ass up quick, but when he turned to face him, his face was struck with the barrel of Blow's handgun forcing him to fall.

"Damn Dog! What the fuckkk?" he stumbled over his words from the hard strike. His head was thumping like a heart under a stethoscope and the bloody gash across his nose and eye was forcing Teddy's shit to swell.

"Shut up bitch ass nigga!" Blow hissed viciously. "Where the fuck is my money, nigga? You tried me and pulled grimy like I wouldn't find you. Lie to me and you die here. Where that fucking dough at?" He mashed the gun forcefully into his forehead.

Piss shot up from his boxers and the way he rotated his head back and forth showed that he was still in wonderland. "Bruh, I didn't have a choice...You were gonna cross me, nigga. Jabari comes up dead. You try to kill lil bru and I had to be next. I didn't know what to do," he spat with a slur.

"Bitch nigga, I said that it was gonna be split and even the money we didn't have yet. You slid out with the whole bag and cut me the fuck out pussy." Blow reached down to his pockets and snatched the bundles of cash out aggressively. Both fronts were stuffed with blue Benjamin's, and the nigga even had a small stash in his right sock. Blow confiscated the Frank Muller watch from his wrist and struck him with the gun a second time.

"I said where is my shit, Teddy!" His eyes grew wide with impatience.

Exhaling heavily, Teddy balled up his face with fear. "I spent it, man. The half I left for you got stolen before I could bring it back. Real shit. That's why I never showed back up, Blow. You had me shook, man."

The first slug tore through his chest and the next one smashed against the side of his head, placing him on slump for life.

Bloc! Bloc!

His body forced a final breath and the bowel he released lingered with the air in a matter of seconds.

"Shake that fuck nigga!" Blow spat before turning around to leave the bathroom.

Stepping back out in the hallway, the bar grew louder, and he placed his pistol back on his hip before doing a quick self-check. Walking through the small path, he made it back to the front of the bar and left the building faster than a portrait thief in Paris. The adrenaline was pumping like a motherfucker and he had to make his way from that side of town before anyone got a clear view of what he was pushing.

Jumping back in his whip, he cranked up and left the parking lot speeding like a bat out of hell. After he dashed across the intersection next to the gas station. He pulled out his phone to call Brandon. Scrolling to his number, he dialed it, placing it up to his ear.

"Hello?"

"Listen, Brandon, I need you to come meet me right away. Man, I think it's some fishy stuff going on. We need to meet up so we can be on point. Real shit." Blow was breathing heavily through his line.

"What's going on, man? Why you breathing so hard?" Brandon asked in a feeble tone. He instantly knew that Blow was stirring some fuck shit.

"Don't speak too much, lil bro. Meet me at the spot in thirty minutes. If we ain't outta Cali tonight, we might be getting sent to the Feds in Alaska by morning. Come now," he stressed.

"A'ight man. I'm not on that side of town, but I'll come, bro," Brandon agreed in order to get him off the phone.

"Bet!" Blow hung up.

Brandon drove down the street of Cynthia's bakery with a curious feeling in his gut about the phone call he just received. Blow was moving extremely weird. After hearing about the death of Leo made him think he was plotting on flipping out and killing everyone who was involved. A meet up was damn sure out of the question. After getting a light distance down the street, the sight of a bright fire could be seen glowing brightly through his Durango's windshield. The more he approached it, he began to realize that the blaze of fire was Cynthia's bakery. Stopping his car, he stepped out looking at the small eatery burning in flames. The entire inside was covered with fire, and so much smoke was flying from the windows drifting up with the breeze. His mouth hung open with a look of horror. Her last words from yesterday replayed through his mind and he could tell whatever she needed to say was important. Not even twenty-four hours later, her mother's shop was being torched to the ground. Stumbling to get back in his car, Brandon shut the driver's door and drove past the surrounding cars that stood around in amazement. The sound of fire trucks and ambulances were starting to wail closer. And before he got caught waiting around to die or figure out the strange mystery occurring, he was about to grab whatever necessary to get the fuck out of dodge however possible. Mashing his gas pedal, he thought about heading to Jabari's spot, but quickly changed his mind knowing that Blow would show before the night was out. After a few seconds of driving, a light struck his mind and he quickly bust a right on the next street to head the opposite way.

Chapter 18
Secluded Area
3:34 A.M.

Feeling the large truck come to a halt, Veronica tried her best not to fall face-first from the sudden brake. Her head jumped against the passenger seat headrest. The bodyguard climbed out of his front seat and quickly removed her from the truck. Her vision was still blinded from the last time she had spoken to her father and now she was arriving at a new destination. Her cold feet were slapping against the pavement as the strong ass guard gripped her cuffed hands like she was banished to prison for life. The sound of a steel door could be heard rising from the use of a raggedy chain link and once she entered the medium-sized warehouse, the cold wind pierced her skin like a knife clawing at the center of her tongue. Her feet mashed against a pile of hay as she moved deeper inside the building. Veronica's blinding case was removed giving her site of the field warehouse she stood inside. Her dad, Vinnie, was standing beside a block of hay where he fumbled with his alligator Italian dress shoes. The steam from the cold air was blowing out of his mouth along with the thick cigarette he puffed on roughly. The guard stopped directly in front of a large box machine that was partially covered with a lengthy thick and beige spread.

Tossing out his nicotine stick, he placed his hands into his trench before approaching her. "Veronica, I've been roaming around, and according to what you said, baby, this guy Blow isn't the only one involved that you are aware of. Pumpkin, this is the time to come clean." He held her shoulders to show how important that moment was.

Her lips shook uncontrollably, and her instincts began to realize that shit was about to get deeper than a cut off from the family. Her pride wanted to hold it, but she couldn't. "His nam-eee was Jabar-iii! His brother was with him also. They can't tell you where it is cau-ssee he's dead, daddy," she explained, hoping that he understood.

Vinnie exhaled deeply. "This Jabari person, and his brother, where can I find them?" He shook his head disapprovingly.

"I don't know daddy. I swear. They never told me anything." She sniffled as warm tears stained her pale cheeks.

"Why didn't you tell me this earlier when I asked the first time? You told me that Blow was the only person you knew about Veronica?"

"I-I -was-s scared." Her head shook from side to side. That was the best she could think of and her bladder felt as if it was about to explode.

Vinnie pulled her in for a hug, and whispered in her ear, "You can't lie about things when I ask because that is a betrayal against the ones you love, honey. Your Italian and your honor comes from keeping family first at all times. How can we be a family if you take away from us, honey?" he explained before releasing her. His spirit seemed to calm down and his eyes softened like the way he looked at her when she was just a precious little one running around his home. Kissing her forehead, he snapped a finger and walked away from her without another word. The sound of a loud woodchipper ignited, shredding her heart to pieces. Her eyes grew wide, trying back away from the contraption in front of her.

"Daddy *please*! I'll find it... I can keep looking. Daddy!" she screamed as the large hitman picked her up by the stomach and feet.

Walking her up to the spinning blades of steel, he dumped her inside headfirst. Her screams grew louder than the motor operating the chipper. The sound of her bones cracking like twigs slid through Vinnie's ears before he exited the caged door of the warehouse. His heart wanted to shed a tear for the lovely princess he birthed into the world, but the price for slashing the loyalty of la familia couldn't be scratched away with forgiveness. The loud blade was griding against her torso, mutilating her dead body like a thick piece of cotton. Her legs still shook uncontrollably, but the guards ensured that every part was through the grinder before shutting the machine off.

Hearing the silence fill the air, Vinnie asked his mother in heaven for her strong healing energy about her granddaughter's demise. Lighting another cigarette, he got into the front seat of his Lincoln Navigator and pulled out of the driveway, heading for a new mission. The next stop was to a detective birdie whose father was digging inside the wrong cookie jar.

Chris Green

Chapter 19
Blow's Condo Complex
4:00 A.M.

After waiting for Brandon to pull up to the crib, Blow noticed that he was playing games once his phone began to fly straight to the voicemail. The timid ass little nigga knew how to move quickly because his life was surely about to slide like the rest if he didn't get any valuable info from his lying mouth. If everyone was dead, then a motherfucker wouldn't be able to enjoy the paper just like he couldn't. It was time to play chess and he was the nasty Queen slapping shit across the board from left and right.

Parking his car, he squeezed the last puff of the rolled Sour Diesel marijuana. His eyes were heavy from the Xanax bars he crushed inside of his cold Sprite bottle, and the atmosphere felt as if it was moving at ten miles per hour. The chasing was tiring him out, but stopping wasn't gonna happen until he crossed all T's. In T's he meant tops, and he damn sure wasn't thinking about shirts.

Taking the keys from his ignition, he opened the car door, and slowly took his time to stand up out of the seat. His legs felt like they were floating on air, and the wind sliding across his face had his body feeling like a piece of paper. He knew for a fact about one thing. He was high as a motherfucker, but it looked like two Chinese police officers were walking straight towards him. Blow blinked his eyes, and the image of Mickey and Mikey's psychotic twin faces cleared in his line of sight. He began to reach for his pistol too late. The identical mini carbon 15's the Italian brothers carried raised up towards Blow's face before he could grip the handle. The chamber racking back drained the fake ass high clean out of his system.

"I'll split your face with a full thirty before you spit out two syllables," Mickey's Italian voice warned with malice tracing every word. His brother remained quiet with a firm grip on his semi. One of his eyes fidgeted as if he was anxious to send him away for a meet up to the supreme being.

"What the fuck is this? Y'all motherfuckers don't know me and I ain't did shit. I don't owe you niggas nothing," Blow spat with his hands raising up slowly.

"Speak when spoken to and keep your body stiffer than a piece of frozen meat. The pool area. Make your way there. Swiftly." Mickey pointed the barrel of his weapon in the direction.

Blow didn't want to go out like a bitch to some white people, but the military weapons in their hands forced his nuts to tuck for that special occasion. Keeping his lips sealed, he stumbled into the gated entrance of his home. Taking the pathway around to the enclosed pool in the back, Blow spotted a group of men posted in the area and knew that someone was really calling shots to have him ambushed by a group of cop-looking ass niggas. He pondered on Brandon setting him up with the law, but he knew that the young one was too spooked to get caught in the mix of anything, so Blow's mind wandered at a money machine pace about the men he was currently dealing with.

Entering the small, gated pool, Mickey and Mikey walked him smoothly over to their father who sat back on the beach chair with a bag of plain Lay's potato chips in his hand. Six suited Italians beamed their eyes on his face with dirty expressions. Their only job was to wait for Frankie's call, and the rest would change anybody's life within a flash. The boss man stared at Blow while munching on the last few crumbles inside of the bag. Licking his fingers, he used a napkin to wipe his hands and tossed it at Blow's feet before lighting a slim fresh-picked Cuban cigar. Snapping his fuel lighter shut, he exhaled a cloud of smoke and smiled.

"Good morning sir. I'm so sorry that you have to be all uncomfortable in the pool area of your residence this early. I'm actually sleepy, and truly I wouldn't have never come here if your name wouldn't have slid through the loops in my ears." Frankie waved a hand around as if it was all good.

"I don't know you, my guy. As you can see, I'm Black. I don't deal with shit outside of my race. So maybe you got the wrong guy." Blow smirked before crossing his hands in front of him.

"Oh, I'm quite sure that you're the man I need. Blow, right?" Frankie asked, pointing a gun finger at him. "Yeahh...That's you, and I can tell by the way you swallowed your spit when your name fell from my mouth. It's okay though. You don't have to worry about me playing any games with you. If you answer my question and give the right answer, you're free to go... If you don't..." Frankie chuckled under his breath and took another puff of the cigar.

Blow scratched the bridge of his nose feeling the aura thicken suddenly. Holding his cool, he started processing a way to make a move if necessary. "What in the fuck do you wanna know from me?"

"Easy. Where in the fuck is my fifteen million dollars that you and your little friends swiped from my casino's safe? That fucking question."

Blow's face softened with respect, and the grumble in his belly let him know that the guys in his presence weren't there for a butter smooth conversation. "I never robbed your spot, and I don't mean no disrespect when I say this, but if I did strike that good for millions, I wouldn't be in the same spot waiting for some unknown ass face to pull up and take it back from me. Now, do I know about the word going around the city of who could pull a stunt so clever? Maybe... It's small around this area and you can't shit too loud without the entire hood knowing about it three minutes later," Blow spoke with confidence.

"How about you give me what I need, so I can push out of this old ass chair to reclaim my currency?"

One of the Italians pulled two pairs of long shackles from a black bag and held them in his palms. Blow's eyes roamed down to the four heavy cinder blocks resting on the ground.

"The dude you're looking for is named Jabari and he's currently laying in a casket from my knowledge, but the one who's probably still holding your money is his little brother. His name is Brandon from the Hagginwood neighborhood. He's barely seventeen and maybe you'll have a better chance finding him 'cause my luck has been on ice," Blow tossed a curve in the game to draw the heat from him.

"Jabari and Brandon...Hagginwood area?" Frankie mumbled with a slow nod. "How do I know that you just aren't rubbing my nuts to ease the pain in my ass, kid? It seems like your name is ringing bigger bells than any other name that's been given?"

"All I have is my word. If you want your money, you gotta stroll through that dangerous ass hood and get it back. No point of me lying about money that's not being spent from my pockets," he shot back.

Frankie saluted his arrogance, but it wasn't enough to convince the Don. Waving at two of his trusted henchmen, one grabbed his arms from behind and placed a pair of shackles on his wrists. The other tall Sicilian muscle locked on to his head and rolled a fresh piece of duct tape around his mouth to secure his pleading remarks. He struggled with the two dudes to put up a fight, but a quick gut check from one of his twin's guns forced the air to cave down in his legs. His eyes weakened and watered from the excruciating pain. That move allowed the last guard to clamp the ankle shackles around the cinder blocks before attaching them to his feet. Dragging him closer to the poolside, he jerked while ranting muffled slurs through the dense material that was over his mouth. Pushing the concrete slabs over the edge, Blow's body tumbled over with them also sinking straight to the bottom of the twelve-foot section. The square rocks could be heard clinking the bottom and his body would remind you of a shark attack gone wrong if you didn't know that steel restraints had a hold of him. Blow's head and legs rocked at an awkward rhythm as the ruthless Italians stood above watching him suffer like the dog and liar he was. Trails of blood began to stream from his nose and Frankie was preparing himself to leave once the movements of the water calmed to a sleeping body of water.

"I need Vinnie to check in with us, guys. He searched for this guy all day and we found him in three hours. Someone's dedication is not so ecstatic about finding our missing funds. Let's see what's next from here fellas. Mickey, lead us to our next destination, please. I'm starting to get homesick," Frankie requested as they walked slowly out of the pool's entrance to the front parking lot.

Blow's dead body was hovering around the bottom of the water and it was positive that he may not get found until sunrise. Fate was something a joker couldn't even cheat, and the look of defeat was embedded on his face. It was the look of torment. One that told you he was already being crushed between the depths of hell. Frankie wanted to pass on that feeling until he didn't have any involved targets walking the face of his earth.

Chris Green

Chapter 20
Hagginwood
Ronald's House

Rolling over out of his sleep, he scrunched his eyes from the small burst of sun rays that snuck through the blinds. The empty beer bottles next to him that was drunk last night and the small half a pound of weed that was stashed in the kitchen's cabinet was missing about a full ounce. His head was beating like a fistfight, and it was more than likely from all the rolled blunts he smoked to calm his nerves until nightfall passed. Standing up, he headed for the bathroom and took a quick piss. The thought of Cynthia and Victoria ran across his mind. Once he flushed the toilet and walked out, Brandon immediately tried to call her phone number. Twelve missed calls were floating at the top of his screen from Blow, but that was the last nigga he wanted to speak to. Victoria's phone gave the same results it did almost ten hours ago. An auto voice recording started to play. The end button was clicked before he tossed it down on the kitchen table. Victoria's disappearance of out the blue shook the hell out of him, and even gossiping hood talkers was exposing the secrets about the major caper they struck for in Nevada. Without any family to lean on sincerely, his options on what to do came up short.

Instead of thinking too hard, he decided to go ahead and catch a fast shower before jumping on the road to keep moving. The small amount of cash would hold him over until he crossed paths of a blessing to make it from out of the state. If Blow happened to slide past his presence trying to pull a slick one, he was prepared to use the .357 revolver that he found under Jabari's old mattress after searching the crib from top to bottom the night before.

Grabbing some old towels and wrinkled T-shirt, he slid inside the bathroom and locked the door. The shower was started, and he placed the gun and clothes directly on the toilet seat before jumping in the mildly hot water. Using some shampoo to cleanse himself, he closed his eyes and allowed the steam to ease his tension. If only Jabari was able to give him advice at the time. It was for sure that his words would make everything so clear. The trust dog tag that Jabari purchased for him dangled around his neck as if was talking in silence, but Brandon's mind just couldn't ponder on what step to take.

* * *

Mickey and Mikey drove slowly up the suspected street they were searching for in search of the direct home. The car stopped partially in the middle of the street. When Mickey looked across to the right side and spotted Brandon's dad's house, they studied the view of the home. They glanced back at each other to see if the agreement about being the correct one was mutual. Making sure to park a few doors down before killing the engine, Mickey cocked back his strap and stepped out slowly. Mikey did the same but screwed a silencer on his gun while leaning in his doorway. Nodding to his twin, Mikey led the way by trailing smoothly up the sidewalk.

Chapter 21
Sacramento Police Department
Detective Shannon Kegg's Unit #6
Special Forces

Shannon scrolled down the list of call logs that her sister had stored on her sim chip. The recent numbers and people she had been speaking to were a few bank loaners, locksmiths for steel doors, and a bunch of different lines that would only make you get frustrated after picking through the first thirty-six of 'em. Shannon had gone far as even checking the photos and email's thoroughly to find a hint of what she needed in order to prove what her mind already expected.

The knock at the door grabbed her attention and her assistant, Detective Johnson, peeked his head inside with a thumbs up. "I found the address you needed. It's off a street over in Hagginwood. 1397 or something like that. It's a brown and white home that belonged to Mr. Ronald Salters before he passed a few years back." Johnson raised an eyebrow.

"Hagginwood. That's a big area. It's a polluted area and finding the home shouldn't be easy when you got people who wanted to run their mouth for free." Shannon put on her black jacket in a small rush. She needed to contact Brandon for a small talk before a problem crept upon his head. The time read nine sixteen in the morning, and the drive was no less than a few minutes from the department if she took the short back streets. Jogging straight for the parking garage. She rushed towards the Black Police cruiser with the Hemi motor inside. Hopping in, she swerved out of the gated bars and flashed straight for the nastiest spot that you couldn't dig out of Sacramento even if you tried. Slapping on her sirens to disregard all the stoplights, she pressed the gas accelerating up to 89 miles an hour. Her mind was locked in on the task at hand and that was finding out who held the power over all the buttons that were being pushed in her city. It was time to find out and place a hold on the unknown for the last time.

* * *

Trying to look through the windows of the home. The twin brothers began to search for the easiest way to enter without alerting the neighbors. "Walk down into the back of the home and see if the basement has a door that we can slide inside. Check windows, and try to keep the noise down," Mikey whispered over in his ear.

Smiling evilly, he smirked before cutting through the grass to head out the back. Mikey tried to twist the front doorknob and had no justice. Observing what kind of keyhole that it possessed, he pulled a thin metal utensil from his pants pocket and dropped down to one knee. Sliding the instrument inside, he used a thin bobby pin to finesse the bolt to open. The ridges of a lock were like squirming through a maze that was getting tighter by the second. Every layer had to be caressed perfectly in order to gain access to its finish mark.

The light click was like music to his ears. Once he turned his wrist, the lock shifted to the right giving him access to what was behind door number one. Rising back to his feet, he removed his Fifty caliber Desert Eagle. The knob was turned, and he was sure to peek inside before sneaking in quiet as a gust of wind. He closed the door behind him.

* * *

Before Shannon reached the street of Ronald's address, she killed the sirens not wanting to raise fear in Brandon's eyes. It was only one last chance he had to save himself or allow everyone that he cared for to be hunted down and killed like a wild animal.

Turning down his street, she pulled down in front of the home and spotted a black Dodge Durango parked in the yard. Unstrapping her seatbelt, she got out of the cruiser and walked up to the home's front porch. The dusty stairs and guard rail was filled with pollen, and it looked nearly like the home was about to stand for its last fight. Shannon reached her hand out to knock, and the door slightly cracked, exposing that someone had recently entered the threshold. Her police issued Ruger was pulled from the holster before she used her foot to lightly push the door open wider.

Chris Green

Chapter 22

The living room of the old school home reeked like a stale and pissy couch that had been kept for over twenty years. Mikey clutched on his gun tightly peeping over into the kitchen. Walking inside, he checked the cabinets for any clues or hidden bags of cash. Finding nothing but a sink of moldy dishes and silverware. He looked out of the window and watched his brother Mickey checking the shed out back.

Deciding to keep moving, He headed for the center hallway. A large master bedroom sat ahead, and it was closed shut. Moving closer, he thought he heard a slight movement and placed an ear to the door. Twisting the knob, he pushed it open and raised his gun around in case someone thought about pulling a slick one. Checking the closet, he came up short. The single mattress was on the floor and a T.V was the only thing that caused the room to feel completely empty.

Turning around, he headed out of the room and pushed further down the hallway. Another room was on the right-hand side and a small oak door sat directly in front of him. His mind said to try the room on the right first, but the steam coming from under the middle room made him realize that a shower was being occupied at that very moment. The sound of water running grew once he inched further up, and whoever was inside didn't know that the phantom himself was lurking in the vicinity for blood. Reaching his hand out for the doorknob, a hard whack from the back of Shannon's pistol stopped him in his tracks. Mikey's body crashed to the floor and his leg shook lightly.

Shannon's heart skipped a beat before posting against a wall. The sound of the back door being closed made her think hastily. Her mind knew that a criminal like the Italian lunatics she was dealing with wouldn't hesitate to murder for their honor and respect.

The sight of him crossing into the living room from the kitchen with his weapon aimed made her stiffen. All his head had to do was rotate, and her ass would be in deep shit. She didn't want to use her gun, but just as she prayed for him to keep moving, he turned, locking eyes with her before she pulled her trigger twice and taking him down.

Boom! Boom!

Brandon jumped harder than a hoe after hearing a gun let loose in his house. Let alone he was in the shower ass naked and that was one of the shittiest of ways to being tricked out of the hood. Reaching out the curtains, he grabbed the clothes and gun from the toilet seat. Rushing to get dressed behind the small plastic cover, he hopped out of the shower and slid back on his shoes.

Shannon was still nervous from firing the shots, but her mind said shoot. Closing in on his body, Mickey's eyes looked up at the ceiling with a frown. The gun wounds on his body leaked a small puddle under him while she was bending down to check for a pulse. The slight second that she bent down was all the chance Brandon needed to make her regret it, zooming past her like a breath of fresh air. Shannon's head raised feeling the strong wind behind her. The back of Brandon's shirt was flapping like the wind and his quick feet were sliding right out of the front door before she could get to her feet. Trying to chase him was like a video game. Every step she took forward was like him making six. By the time she reached the doorway, he had already leaped the porch and jumped in the driver seat of the high-powered Durango.

"Freeze!" Shannon aimed her gun at his back windshield.

Ignoring her command, he floored the gas and jumped the Hemi up to seventy-five, forcing it to slide through the grass to make a getaway. The tires hollered like a hoarse voice child running through the grocery aisle, leaving Shannon in his dad's driveway. He smashed his whip down the street until she disappeared in his rearview. Flushing his way out of the Hagginwood area. He tried to think of where to go, but nothing could come to mind. So many people were looking, so many eyes were watching to spill the beans of his whereabouts, and he didn't want to perish for trusting the enemy. Within days, plenty had died, and the only thing the streets were whispering about was the *City of Kingz* of Sacramento. Jabari's words were starting to fall all over the sloppy mess, and now he cursed himself for not learning more with not trusting his word. "Always follow me, lil bro, and you'll win. Jabari would look him in the eyes before tapping his temple meaning think."

The uneasiness that was causing his emotions to quake stopped immediately and a flashlight erupted through his brainwaves showing him the sloppiest mistake he could have ever made. Being sure that no one was behind him, he busted a sharp right and knew exactly where he could find his peace. He was partially safe at the moment, but after the sun dropped where he could creep. His movements were gonna be selected wisely. If he couldn't find a vision from not having Jabari around, Brandon was gonna make his way back to him. Brandon pondered while breathing in small and short winds. Taking a swig of the half a bottle of Remy Martin Black, he downed four large shots and sat it back down. The feeling of the liquor calmed him somewhat, and it was all he could use to hold him over until he made a move at the accurate time.

Chris Green

Chapter 23
Secluded Warehouse
10:10 A.M.

Vinnie's skin was boiling like a pot of lava as the chains dug into his legs and wrist. The blood rushing to his brain had him nauseous like a trip on a sea boat. His eyes were blindfolded and every time his heart beat, a sharp pain would thump in his temples and chest. His circulation was being cut short, and if he wasn't let loose soon, his body would be stiffer than a worked-out muscle. Feeling a strong hand snatch the cloth from his eyes, he blinked a few times before noticing Frankie and their henchmen standing in front of him. He coughed violently and his eyes were bloodshot red.

"Vinnie, I've had love for you for more than twenty years, and I can actually say that it hurts to see you on the opposite side of the room from me. I gave you the world just like my father did me when I was younger. I'm just not understanding why our stories are not ending differently." He shook his head in shame.

Frankie clasped his hands and grabbed the wooden bat from his foot soldier's hand. "This is a gift that my father gave me when I was fourteen years old. It's still practically brand new. A Louisville slugger. It was a birthday present. My dad succeeded at a lot of things, but there was one matter he didn't take seriously enough. Keeping his words." Frankie grinned before smashing the wooden bat into his nuts.

"Arghh!" He choked on his own breath with a small amount of spit running down his lip. The horrific pain caused stars to twinkle through his pupils and each second felt like he would pass out in his own urine. Vinnie's eyes bulged as the chain swung him gently in the air, and the Italian men standing firm didn't feel any pity for a man that claims to be a boss who takes no excuses for the Mob. The loss in Vegas was totally his fault, but Frankie wanted to be

163

fair when it came to giving him a way out. Vinnie fixed his mouth to feel that he could get the money back, but since they arrived in Cali, nothing had occurred but murder and the law trying to shut them out from the limits of Sacramento. That alone forced his hand to make an example of whether a man was family or not.

Frankie handed the bat in his hand over to a guard and huffed. "I need to locate my boys and order the deaths of every major cop in this city. I lost my money; they'll lose their families. We're even until we break even," he ordered for one of the men to make happen.

"Sure thing, Frankie." He stepped to the side to make a call.

"Vinnie, I'm afraid this is the time where I depart from the death house. It's a fifty-gallon barrel of piranhas that's waiting patiently for you, and I don't wanna stop those little guys' feast," Frankie explained as a few of his men rotated Vinnie's body over the large green can.

The top was shaking like a vibrator. Once it was removed, one of the fish nearly hopped four feet in the air waiting to be fed. Vinnie dropped a single tear with a straight face.

"I'm sorry, Frankie. I only wanted to make you proud about maintaining the family business. I love you, man," he forced the words from his gut.

"I love you too, pal." He nodded and started to disperse towards the exit. The sound of the chain releasing forced a womanly scream from Vinnie before he dropped inside the giant bucket of small man-eaters. The water was bubbling as the fish bounced around on their morning meal. A middle finger from Vinnie's right hand bubbled to the surface floating gently on top. The thick red blood made it hard to see the damage the demons really did, but it was quite understood. No one was safe from the bounds of Frankie's touch. No one knew exactly how heartless the Italian man could be, but if ordering the death of his grandmother for saying fuck the family wasn't scary enough, imagine how he moved with a person who didn't share the same blood. Death was mixed inside of his coffee every morning, and feelings was a trait that he never had a chance to experience. The world was meant for balance and control. It's the reason why you had levels to living. His rank was beyond the most, and if you didn't want your name scratched from the board. It would take a major reason. One that had to be beneficial to the legislators of the table or the punishment would be devastating.

* * *

Sunset Lawn Memorial Cemetery
9:55 P.M.

Brandon finally arrived at Sunset after driving around the interstate and city for the past nine hours. His uneasy ass paranoia was making him feel like every whip that drove behind the car was following him to the destination. He refused to go for the tricks and fall victim so instead of jumping off the correct exit. He flipped and rode the highway for hours until he felt comfortable enough to slide off. The dark cemetery was easy to move around, and it was completely empty allowing his aura to be at ease. Sliding over to the section where Jabari was buried, he climbed out of the car and tucked the .357 handgun into his jacket pocket. A hoodie was over his head and the creepy-ass sound from the grass crunching under his feet felt like a nigga was following him. Looking around nervously, he crossed over the small field and spotted the large pile of dirt where Jabari was placed into the ground. Once he reached the area, he stood in silence for a second.

The tombstone hadn't been fitted into the ground yet, and the scenery only made him want to drop a face full of tears before he could even force himself to let his brother know that he was dearly missed. He knew that liquor was a bad mixture when trying to cope with death in a family, so he was gonna be sure to stay clear from any strong drinks after that day. His mind was running like a grey-hound bus that had been rerouted seven times.

"What's up, Bari?" He squatted down next to the pile of dirt that was rising slightly out of the ground. "I know I failed, and you probably mad at me. I was never ready, and I pushed you to really think I was." Brandon sighed while fumbling with a skimpy blunt of weed.

The sky was black as the soul of Satan, but the white clouds swirling around inside of it forced a feeling that shit was never gonna be perfect. It could seem like a dark room was closing in on you when something was happening, but you never understood that you were the light the entire time. Nothing could stop a man from finding his way, but his own actions. The misguidance of feelings. It was a number one destructor. That was the way Brandon felt about the suffering he was taking in at the moment.

"I know that if I would have listened to you more, I would have a different understanding of many things. The entire crew has fallen to our demise on the strength of that nigga Blow just like you said. You warned me about him, but I didn't see it until it was too late. Now I'm stuck without you, all about some punk ass bread." Brandon rubbed his eyes and lit the little joint for a puff.

The wind started to blow a tad bit harder, forcing him to hold his hoodie on. After all the death that took place, it was him standing alone with no crutches to stand on. Shaking his head, he cried lightly for the desperate moment. He never felt so lost, so defeated. It was straining him being left alone, and the shit made him realize that he truly needed to follow before he could be a leader.

"Tell me what to do, Bari. Just give me advice this last time 'cause I'm losing it, bro. I can't beat everyone." He dropped down on his knees exhaling deeply. A small thunder struck the sky and the casket cover that sat above him started to rock back and forth like it would tilt over at any second. Brandon closed his eyes, and his mind cleared all the weakness from his brain. He knew it took courage to move like Jabari and being a coward was a trait that he would've never accepted. He was his exact replica. The chain on his neck dangled and the diamond-encrusted tag started to spin in a circle until the glistening words "Trust" twinkled in his eyes.

"Just remember to always follow me, lil bro, and you'll always win. Follow me and you'll always win. Follow me and you'll always win." Jabari's words repeated in his head until his eyes shot open faster than a rocket.

Rising up slowly with a stunned face, he mumbled it to himself, "Keep your eyes open and watch. Follow me and you'll always win." He gasped as his breathing started to pick up.

The sound of something hitting the ground forced Brandon to jerk his head to the right. A white man dressed in a dirty brown dickie suit was staring at him with a surprised face. He was the keeper of the cemetery and the same one who trailed around cleaning up on the day of Jabari's burial. Brandon didn't know what his next move was gonna be because he stood in the same spot staring without a word. Tilting his hat, a wide smile spread across his face.

"Well, it's about damn time. I'm rich!" He laughed with an annoying raspy tone. Stuffing the shovel down in the dirt, the man removed the gloves, sitting them on the handle. "Good luck kiddo." He broke off into a light sprint across the grass. "I quitttt! I quitttt! Wooooo!!!" he cheered, disappearing across the dark hill to wherever destination it was that he had in mind.

Brandon tried to replay what the hell just happened to cause the old creepy guy scared the fuck out of him. The statement he made was beyond weird, and now he was rich in the back of his mind. He was waiting, and after his sign was revealed, nothing could stop him from knowing something that everyone else didn't.

The rumbles in the sky were ignored again, and now his thinking cap was going in overload. The closed casket funeral was pre-arranged, and he still never got a chance to see his brother's face one last time before he was taken. His promise was to always follow. No matter what. Even if it meant to the grave along with him. "Follow me and you'll always win," Jabari's voice sounded as if it were standing directly beside him.

Rushing over to the shovel, he placed on the work gloves and glanced at the time on the watch that read 10:17. Huffing a hard breath of air, Brandon slammed the shovel into the dirt tossing a large pile to the side. Digging in again, his heart tingled with a slight assurance that his mind was working clearer than he expected. That drive alone made him start to dig faster. His pace began to speed up, and after five minutes of moving with a consistent rhythm, he drowned out the shit around him and lost it. The shovel was moving quicker and sweat started to form at the tip of his forehead, but memories of their childhood began to flash before his eyes. The abuse from his dad on the late nights where Jabari didn't make it home. Days of the foster home and staying with friends of the family. Out of all the years they suffered, he always ensured that if he paid attention to shit before moving off how he felt, it would always be as clear as transparent paper. The trance he was in stirred his mind in a warp, and after forty-five minutes of non-stop dirt slanging, Brandon realized the hard surface he smacked against next was the door of his brother's coffin. Clearing the thick layer of sticky mud off the top, he gazed at it with a painful ache sliding through his chest cavity. Sliding his finger through the crease of the casket, he inhaled and snatched it open. The sight of what his eyes saw stopped his heart completely. A tear was about to fall, but he caught it and closed his eyes tightly as if it were a dream. Reopening them, He stared down at the nicely decorated space, but Jabari's body was damn sure not laying comfortably inside of that bitch. Reaching under the small fabric sheets and pillows, he snatched the entire section out revealing another shocker. He paused before picking up a large clear bundle of blue hundreds wrapped in plastic. A white piece of paper was resting on top of another bundle. Brandon unfolded it and read it slowly. "It took you long enough!" A pair of coordinates sat at the far bottom obviously giving him directions to another mystery. His heart was pumping so hard that he literally felt like he was about to blackout. Catching his balance, he glanced at a good forty more bundles of freshly printed dinero. The loud thunder sounded again above him, but this time, the rain began to drizzle lightly.

Climbing his ass out of the dirty ass ditch, he ran full speed back to his car. Opening the front door, he popped the trunk and snatched two of the large packing bags inside. Wasting no time, he sped back up the hill tripping on his face. A small amount of grass slid into his mouth, but he kept it moving like it didn't faze him. The large hole was collecting most of the rain, and before shit got messy, he was about to clear that bitch out.

Heading back inside, he started to stuff the first bag neatly as possible to fit everything that he could. The blocks of dough were plentiful, and all he could think about was choking the fuck out of his brother whenever he found out exactly what the fuck was going on. It didn't take longer than five minutes for him to fill one tote with twenty packages. Using his arm strength, he grabbed the next one and did the exact same thing. The rain grew harder, and the thunder was booming back-to-back inside his eardrum. Once he finally got the bag filled, he took a few seconds to catch his breath while the rain caressed his face. Pushing the bag up top. he used the last of his strength and drug himself to the top. Rolling over on his back, he glared in the sky trying to regain his energy. Once he had enough stamina to stand, He tried to reach down for the bags.

The large slap from the shovel across his head sent him straight back to the ground.

Whack!

His body folded like paper and when his lids shut this time, they didn't open back up.

* * *

Five Hours Later

Brandon could finally feel his lungs open up giving him a fresh breath of air. The top of his head ached terribly, and it felt like it took forever to open up his eyes. By the time he was wide awake from the unconscious slumber, a smooth bell rang at a low tone. "Only a few more hours, sir," a woman's voice spoke through a speaker box.

Brandon tried to shake his head in order to shake off the weakness clawing at his bones. Rolling his head sideways, he stared out of the window wondering where the hell he was headed. The area he passed through looked strange, and he damn sure never saw a spot that had so many foggy ass streets. Blinking twice, Brandon soon noticed that those foggy roads were the thick clouds that were over ten thousand feet in the air.

The adrenaline he had at the cemetery was finally rushing back, and now he was checking out everything that was going on around him. In a seat, sitting to the side of him about fifteen feet away, a white man who was suited in a black F.B.I Agent jacket was typing away on a laptop. His smooth hair was combed straight to the back and he obviously felt Brandon waking up because he turned to face him just as he started to move around. His hands were cuffed, and a seatbelt was strapped around him to ensure that he didn't fall from the chair.

"Glad to see you're awake." He nodded and jumped back to his work.

Brandon's mind instantly went to the money that he just found inside of the cemetery. "Where is my cash, and if you were gonna lock me up, why didn't I have my rights read to me like the law stated?" he asked, trying to peep the white man's mind.

The agent smirked. "There was no need to read any rights."

"What!" Brandon grew louder. "What the fuck is going on? You just place me in handcuffs and I'm waking up on a plane, yet there is nothing that you're supposed to alert me with. Can I at least know what the fuck I'm being charged with?"

"Obviously, not listening."

Brandon shuffled in the cuffs with frustration. "Damn!"

The athletic ass surfer cop was done paying him any attention, and a plane was carrying him to an unknown destination against his will. Money damn sure wasn't illegal in America, and if the police had a major case on him involving the FEDS, he would already be booked into a private facility on twenty-four-hour lockdown. The luxury G550 Gulfstream jet was exquisite. Custom made marble floors and countertops for the kitchen area. The bathroom was designed with the same material. One bedroom was available, and the minibar was filled with a variety of beverages and fruits for at least a week round trip. A subzero fridge was stuffed with a great amount of food, and the tension was too settled to feel like Brandon was about to be taken in by the C.I.A. He knew that people were talking about the recent business, but hoped none of it was able to fall back against him. Realizing that he wasn't going anywhere until he landed, he closed his eyes back and drifted into think mode. It didn't take more than ten minutes, and he was back asleep from the smooth coaster in the air.

* * *

The plane was in the air for so long that Brandon never felt it land, nor did he feel the white Agent standing over him with a smile.

"We've landed. I hate that I gotta put it back on, but I have no other choice." He shrugged.

"What? Why the fuck you hiding me under a potato sack, man? I'll give you whatever in order to settle the dispute with whoever is out for me. Just let me get my bread and you can make your own price," Brandon tried to bargain.

"Listen man. I can't help that I follow the rules," he declined, shoving it roughly over his head.

"Ayeee! Aye man somebody fucking help me. I'm being kidnapped!" Brandon started acting like a true idiot knowing that it was over with for escaping whatever was in store for him.

The agent held him with a stronghold, but his jerking and flopping around became aggravating instantly. Sighing, he pinched a pressure point on the side of his neck putting him straight to sleep. Once Brandon's body went limp, he was thrown over the F.B.I agent's shoulder and walked off the plane.

Walking down the leveled plank, the smell of fresh water and flowers danced around the air delicately. The private airport was secluded, and the sight of a Black H-3 Hummer was parked with a heavily armed driver standing beside it. Once the agent reached the vehicle, he placed Brandon in the backseat, strapping him back down. Quickly going to retrieve the recovered money from the MGM Casino, he slowly walked it back to the truck and tossed it inside. Shaking the assassin's hand for a job completed, the Fed handed over a manila folder with his payment and jumped in the front seat. Starting the engine, he smashed off through the lengthy landing space. Making it to the entrance for the cars, he swerved out of the lot and passed a green airstrip sign that read: ''Welcome to Rio''.

Chris Green

Chapter 24
Rio de Janeiro, Brazil
Beachfront Mansion

Feeling the large truck come to a quick stop, Brandon tensed up. The agent climbed from the car removing the bags first. The entrance of the beautiful seven-bedroom home was beyond the average shit that one would see on a television screen. Bundles of rose gardens and lilies filled the area with an irrigation system for all areas. A total of four luxurious cars were aligned across the smooth pavement as if they had never been moved since they were purchased. One was a true collector's edition. The Silver Porsche 911 with original custom tires, and leather black seats. The dual pipes on the back were low to the ground, and tints were placed around the sides to give more of an offset look to the raging horse Ryder. The house was white aligned with a trimming of light beige circling around every detail the eyes could see. Once he made his way inside to drop off the fetti, he made it back to the car, pulling Brandon out of the backseat. Holding him by the arm, he led him through the parking lot until they reached the threshold of the enormous crib. Once they stepped in, the agent's shoes were clicking against the shiny tile floor and the chandeliers dancing gently above them caused their reflections to bounce off the ceiling. Making it to the center hallway, he removed the bag from Brandon's head.

Mugging the pig with a curled lip, he noticed the clean ass spot he was standing in and started to gaze around at all the exclusive shit. Paintings were spaced out along the walls. Along with different antiques from the Black struggle of African Americans. A double door leading to an outside balcony was wide open. The hue of the purple and blue sky made Brandon gasp from the sight.

Victoria was walking through the hallway in a conversation with her mother, Cynthia, and the new chef. She happened to look

175

up at him standing with a shocked face and smiled from ear to ear. Walking over to him, she embraced a hug on him tightly.

"It's great to see you. I started to think you weren't gonna make it." She took another look at him.

"Oh my, Victoria. We need to shop for better plants," Cynthia called her over before he could even muster a word.

"I'll see you after you get settled, you know how new guests are when they move in." She laughed and headed straight over to her mother.

The agent stood behind him with a straight face, tapping his foot gently on the floor.

"Victoria?" he whispered thinking that he may have been dreaming.

The sound of a woman coming down the steps grabbed his attention. Her tone sounded too familiar, and not one time did he allow his eyes to close until she appeared down the second-floor staircase. He couldn't help but take a small step forward, even though his hands were still cuffed. Her hair was neatly pressed. She was dressed in a beautiful white Marc Jacobs sundress with a pair of slides to match. A coating of light makeup was on her face, and she even smiled once her eyes landed on him. The cellphone that she had up to her ear was instantly lowered.

"Oh my God! Brandonnnn! Hey momma's baby!" she yelled like he had been off to the military before squeezing the hell out of him. "Why are you in handcuffs? What did you do?" Her eyes gazed at him curiously.

"Mama?" He ignored her question, nearly wanting to cry. "You said my name right."

"Why wouldn't I, darling. You're my baby, ain't it?" She winked, planting a kiss on his forehead.

Brandon was lost for words, but the smile he wore said it all. "What's going on mama? Where is Jabari?" he asked, confused about the weird-ass twilight zone he stepped into.

Just as she was about to tell him, the balcony from the back porch opened up, and a pair of suede blue J.M Weston loafers stepped up inside. The white tailored slacks on his body matched his blue fitted Armani exchange silk shirt. The wavy hair was shining, and that million-dollar smile was one that he couldn't forget even if they placed them on a different planet.

Brandon's face balled into a tight smile. "You evil smart bitchh! You set me up," he cursed with a frown.

"Well, that's my cue to let y'all speak." Ms. Salters resumed her call, walking off.

Jabari stepped closer to his brother, and the agent wasted no time releasing him from the handcuffs. Rubbing his wrists, Brandon eyed the agent one last time before stepping face to face with his brother.

"Why?"

"Why?"

Jabari took off his dark lens sunglasses and tilted his head. "Because this is what you wanted Brandon. I offered you a way to be free from that lifestyle, to stay in school, and let me do the groundwork in order to make sure your life is set. This is what you wanted, right?" Jabari was looking him in the eyes waiting for an answer.

Brandon pondered on the hardships he was experiencing throughout the last few days. The death of loved ones. Treachery between friends over money, and remarks. The responsibilities of keeping order, and promises was deep, and that was the lesson Jabari was trying to teach him. If you wanted to be the leader of what you love to do, glow with it so that a motherfucker knew who was in charge. If your *mind* wasn't on leadership and you were following just from being enticed by the hype, it meant that nothing was bound to prosper for your lack of domination and belief.

"I just wanted to make you happy, bro. I'm not good at shit else." Brandon sighed in disappointment.

"You have to worry about what makes you happy, Champ. The reason I moved quietly was to protect the whispers. You needed the experience. This life is harder than you think and there are meaner people in the world than just hood niggas from the block. This can slide from different walks of government from Police Chiefs, Governors, Presidents, and even Kings of different countries. They all play positions on the world's chessboard and if you want to out beat them, you gotta know how hard and when to move. You were born a King in that city, and you'll continue to remain one for life," Jabari said before putting back on his glasses.

"How come?" Brandon questioned to be sure.

"Because no one can stamp the things I've done and escape without ruining shit in the process. Our forty acres and a mule is no longer needed. We already surpassed it and accomplished the parts that the blind still have yet to know about."

Brandon grinned from ear to ear and nodded. His eyes happened to gaze back at the agent who smirked slyly. "Man, what's up with this guy here? When did you start respecting and working with the cops?"

Jabari laughed loudly before giving his friend a brotherly hug. "When they're able to know me from the heart, and not the badge or my last name."

"What the hell is that supposed to mean?"

"Brandon, you really don't know who he is? Try to look a little closer." Jabari stood next to him cheesing.

The appearance of the super-Agent wasn't any different from the rest. He was fit and in great shape. He sported long hair with a light trimmed mustache and beard. Plus, he only spoke when spoken to. Nothing was coming to mind, and Brandon always figured cops were used to being very uptight.

"Nah, nobody that I remember."

"The agent exhaled and dug in his pocket. Pulling out a pair of thick eyeglasses, he placed them on his face with a geeky smile.

"Steven!" he mumbled leaning in closer to him.

"Well, the department calls me Agent Thirty-four now," he said in a nerdy tone.

"Yooo, what the fuck is going on?" Brandon said in disbelief.

"Life," Jabari replied before grabbing the Rag and Bone duffle sitting against the staircase wall. Handing it over to Steven. He shook his hand firmly. "One million as promised, brother. If I need you, I'll be in touch."

"Always Bari. I'm only playing my position." He patted his best friend's shoulder and headed for the door. Before he walked through the front corridor, he turned around. "Hey, what are you gonna do about the Sandy button?"

Jabari laughed hearing the name he used. "I was gonna make good graces. I just have to get the time."

"Well now would be good, 'cause she's out front." Steven chuckled before throwing up his hands.

"What?" Jabari's entire expression changed. "Steven, I know you didn't bring that crazy-ass girl down here with you?"

"I didn't. She followed me," he lied, stepping out the entrance of the home.

"Give me a minute, just make ya'self at home Brandon," he said heading behind his friend. Once he reached the door, he spotted Shannon stepping out of a white B.M.W truck. A white Tory Burch dress clung on to her luscious body tighter than babies gripping a daddy's leg. Her smooth, milky, white skin was glistening for attention with a pair of white Louise et Cie heels clicking on her feet. A black Rachel Comedy bag was on her shoulder, and a white ribbon was tied around the long blonde ponytail that laid down her back. Her blue eyes were draped with a small amount of mascara, her rough ass still had the handle of her gun poking from the purse.

Jabari watched Steven climb into the huge Hummer and winked his eyes before pulling off. By the time he stepped off the mansion's doorstep, Shannon was meeting him. Her braless breast sat up and her light pink lips were a deadly fatal attraction. Jabari's eyes rolled up and down her body. He instantly flashed back to their first encounter. The way she creamed all over him in agony. It was a pleasure at its finest, but there was something that still had to be settled.

"Hello, Detective Shannon."

"Jabari," she replied with a passionate look in her eyes.

"I know that there are some things that need to be explained according to my sloppy friend, Steven, but I never knew that you were here. Of course, you can't fault me for the last encounter be-ing that you were chasing me." He scratched his head while drifting his sight away from her.

"There is," Shannon agreed with a serious face.

"I would allow you to stay, but of course my lady and her mom are getting settled also."

"You mean them?" She nodded to the three women heading out on a mission. They all were climbing inside the new Ferrari for a test drive into town.

"Hey, Jabari. We're leaving for a little girl's night out. We're shopping until we drop. I got the card, don't wait up." His mother giggled as she, Victoria, and Cynthia climbed inside, started the music, and swerved out the driveway like a pack of wolves.

Jabari was speechless for a second with a finger in the air.

Shannon's eyes and head rotated to see if it would spill, but of course, he froze. "I'll be in the guest room. We can talk there." She strutted past him with her ass slanging side to side.

It was a big problem at hand and it damn sure didn't involve being arrested. There was a game of guessing that needed to be reimbursed, and Shannon wasn't taking no for an answer. Thinking about the way shit unfolded, Jabari rubbed his hands together. In order to be a leader, you have to see if one could follow. He smiled before heading inside.

* * *

One Year Later
Pomona, California

Pulling her 2018 Chevy Malibu inside the four-bedroom townhome, Strawberry grabbed the Wal-Mart shopping bag from the passenger seat before stepping out of the car. A nice pink fitting sundress had her cheeks bouncing around like a mind in its own thoughts. It had been a while since leaving Sacramento. After everybody started falling in the grave, she decided to make her new path on starting fresh. Checking the mailbox before she headed up the driveway, she was about to prepare a small dinner and wake up early for her new nursing job. It was a new chance at finding a hobby she could grow to love. Jingling her hand to find the house key, she noticed that the door was slightly ajar. Taking a step back, she pushed it open slowly, thinking that a burglar might have made their way inside. Nothing seemed to be destroyed and silence filled the air. Walking in further, she spotted a large brown FedEx box sitting on her kitchen table. A white blank envelope was taped at the top. Strawberry scanned for the sender's name and couldn't locate one. Her address wasn't even attached to the box which made it more awkward. Sitting down her purse, she grabbed a small cutting knife and split the plastic open. Popping the seals, she nearly fainted from the stacks of cash that was aligned inside. Making sure it wasn't a prank, she flipped through a bundle of bills inspecting it thoroughly. The bank must have made a severe mistake because math was a sweet subject through school. It was damn near a million or more bucks stuffed inside, and a scary-ass feeling started to flow in her head.

Snatching the envelope from under the Scotch tape, Strawberry opened it up. "I never forgot about you!" she read it aloud.

Confusion was still taking over, and who wouldn't forget about who? It didn't make sense to her. A loud thud from upstairs piqued her interest, and now she was sure that someone was damn sure in her crib. Grabbing the meat cleaver from above the stove wall, Strawberry walked smoothly around to the steps that lead to the second floor. That's when she noticed another folded piece of paper on the last step. Picking it up, this one read differently. "Bring yo ass upstairs. Rule number two, never keep me waiting."

The note instantly raised her antennas, and only one nigga could ever make rules when it came down to a boss bitch like herself. That possibility was out the window because that one man she loved dearly was six feet under. So, either somebody wanted to die, or Heather's ass hit the lottery and didn't have anything better to do besides toy around.

Strawberry paced up the steps with the slasher in hand. She was clutching that bitch like Jason, and a motherfucker whole tapeline was getting slapped off if they jumped the wrong way. The top of the steps didn't take long to reach. When she heard the sound of water running inside of her bathroom, it was time to show up or show out. Easing down the hall, she grabbed the doorknob and pushed it open. Steam pushed out harder than a train horn. When it started to clear, her mouth fell down to her feet.

Jabari was bathing calmly under the water with the curtains pulled back. Soapsuds slid down his body, and muscles as his eyes were locked in on that tight ass sundress that was still attached to her skin.

"Bari?" She covered her mouth ready to cry.

"I don't even see why you waiting. I'm not here for nothing." He showed that All-American boy smile while groping himself.

Strawberry couldn't help but giggle with happiness. Her tears were only for the joy of seeing him live in the flesh. Starting at the shoulders, she pulled down her dress allowing her large melons to pop out and get some attention. Her flat tummy was next, and of course, the fabric stopped at her thick coke bottle hips. Forcing it over her apple bottom ass, it wiggled out like Jell-o shots before she let it hit the floor. Her shit was still immaculate, and Jabari hounded over her quickly when she entered his personal space. "I told you that I would never forget about you." He was breathing hard and gripping a hand full of ass.

Strawberry panted from his touch. "Well let me welcome you home, King." She smiled, sliding down to her knees. The talking was over, and love wasn't even the word she was about to receive. It was about to be some grown folks fucking, and Jabari was about to make sure of that.

* * *

After three hours of slow pleasure, Strawberry laid against his chest nearly dozing off to sleep. The sound of Jabari's line ringing forced him to lean over and grab it. "Yeah?"

"Hey, my friend, Jabari," Frankie spoke on the line.

Balling up his face, he looked at the number. "I don't have friends. Who the fuck is this?"

"Come on man. How can't you remember the guys' money you took? It's Frankie from the MGM Casino."

A moment of silence fell, and he was just about to hang up.

"Don't end the call. We need to talk. Put your clothes on, I'll wait."

Wondering who was watching him, he slid Berry over and grabbed his jeans and gun.

"I'm sitting outside. We have a debt to settle, but I can make it easy," Frankie warned.

Glancing out the blinds, the large group of Italians sat against their cars with sly grins. "Red rover, red rover, send the King of Sacramento over." He laughed wickedly before the Italian men walked towards the house with their guns drawn...

To Be Continued...
City of Kingz 3
Coming Soon

Submission Guideline

Submit the first three chapters of your completed manuscript to ldpsubmissions@gmail.com, subject line: Your book's title. The manuscript must be in a .doc file and sent as an attachment. Document should be in Times New Roman, double spaced and in size 12 font. Also, provide your synopsis and full contact information. If sending multiple submissions, they must each be in a separate email.

Have a story but no way to send it electronically? You can still submit to LDP/Ca$h Presents. Send in the first three chapters, written or typed, of your completed manuscript to:

LDP: Submissions Dept
Po Box 944
Stockbridge, Ga 30281

DO NOT send original manuscript. Must be a duplicate.

Provide your synopsis and a cover letter containing your full contact information.

Thanks for considering LDP and Ca$h Presents.

Chris Green

Coming Soon from Lock Down Publications/Ca$h Presents

BOW DOWN TO MY GANGSTA
By **Ca$h**
TORN BETWEEN TWO
By **Coffee**
THE STREETS STAINED MY SOUL **II**
By **Marcellus Allen**
BLOOD OF A BOSS **VI**
SHADOWS OF THE GAME II
TRAP BASTARD II
By **Askari**
LOYAL TO THE GAME **IV**
By **T.J. & Jelissa**
IF LOVING YOU IS WRONG... **III**
By **Jelissa**
TRUE SAVAGE **VIII**
MIDNIGHT CARTEL IV
DOPE BOY MAGIC IV
CITY OF KINGZ III
By **Chris Green**
BLAST FOR ME **III**
A SAVAGE DOPEBOY III
CUTTHROAT MAFIA III
DUFFLE BAG CARTEL VI
HEARTLESS GOON VI

City of Kingz 2

By **Ghost**
A HUSTLER'S DECEIT III
KILL ZONE **II**
BAE BELONGS TO ME III
A DOPE BOY'S QUEEN III
By **Aryanna**
COKE KINGS V
KING OF THE TRAP II
By **T.J. Edwards**
GORILLAZ IN THE BAY V
3X KRAZY III
De'Kari
THE STREETS ARE CALLING II
Duquie Wilson
KINGPIN KILLAZ IV
STREET KINGS III
PAID IN BLOOD III
CARTEL KILLAZ IV
DOPE GODS III
Hood Rich
SINS OF A HUSTLA II
ASAD
KINGZ OF THE GAME VI
Playa Ray
SLAUGHTER GANG IV
RUTHLESS HEART IV

Chris Green

By Willie Slaughter
THE HEART OF A SAVAGE III
By Jibril Williams
FUK SHYT II
By Blakk Diamond
TRAP QUEEN
By Troublesome
YAYO V
GHOST MOB II
Stilloan Robinson
KINGPIN DREAMS III
By Paper Boi Rari
CREAM II
By Yolanda Moore
SON OF A DOPE FIEND III
By Renta
FOREVER GANGSTA II
GLOCKS ON SATIN SHEETS III
By Adrian Dulan
LOYALTY AIN'T PROMISED III
By Keith Williams
THE PRICE YOU PAY FOR LOVE III
By Destiny Skai
I'M NOTHING WITHOUT HIS LOVE II
SINS OF A THUG II
By Monet Dragun

LIFE OF A SAVAGE IV

MURDA SEASON IV

GANGLAND CARTEL IV

CHI'RAQ GANGSTAS III

By **Romell Tukes**

QUIET MONEY IV

EXTENDED CLIP II

By **Trai'Quan**

THE STREETS MADE ME III

By **Larry D. Wright**

IF YOU CROSS ME ONCE II

ANGEL III

By **Anthony Fields**

FRIEND OR FOE III

By **Mimi**

SAVAGE STORMS III

By **Meesha**

BLOOD ON THE MONEY III

By J-Blunt

THE STREETS WILL NEVER CLOSE II

By K'ajji

NIGHTMARES OF A HUSTLA III

By King Dream

THE WIFEY I USED TO BE II

By Nicole Goosby

IN THE ARM OF HIS BOSS

Chris Green

By Jamila
MONEY, MURDER & MEMORIES II
Malik D. Rice
CONCRETE KILLAZ II
By Kingpen
HARD AND RUTHLESS II
By Von Wiley Hall
LEVELS TO THIS SHYT II
By Ah'Million
MOB TIES II
By SayNoMore
BODYMORE MURDERLAND II
By Delmont Player

Available Now

RESTRAINING ORDER **I & II**
By **CA$H & Coffee**
LOVE KNOWS NO BOUNDARIES **I II & III**
By **Coffee**
RAISED AS A GOON I, II, III & IV
BRED BY THE SLUMS I, II, III
BLAST FOR ME I & II
ROTTEN TO THE CORE I II III

190

A BRONX TALE I, II, III

DUFFLE BAG CARTEL I II III IV V

HEARTLESS GOON I II III IV V

A SAVAGE DOPEBOY I II

DRUG LORDS I II III

CUTTHROAT MAFIA I II

By **Ghost**

LAY IT DOWN **I & II**

LAST OF A DYING BREED I II

BLOOD STAINS OF A SHOTTA I & II III

By **Jamaica**

LOYAL TO THE GAME I II III

LIFE OF SIN I, II III

By **TJ & Jelissa**

BLOODY COMMAS I & II

SKI MASK CARTEL I II & III

KING OF NEW YORK I II,III IV V

RISE TO POWER I II III

COKE KINGS I II III IV

BORN HEARTLESS I II III IV

KING OF THE TRAP

By **T.J. Edwards**

IF LOVING HIM IS WRONG…I & II

LOVE ME EVEN WHEN IT HURTS I II III

By **Jelissa**

WHEN THE STREETS CLAP BACK I & II III

Chris Green

THE HEART OF A SAVAGE I II
By **Jibril Williams**
A DISTINGUISHED THUG STOLE MY HEART I II & III
LOVE SHOULDN'T HURT I II III IV
RENEGADE BOYS I II III IV
PAID IN KARMA I II III
SAVAGE STORMS I II
By **Meesha**
A GANGSTER'S CODE I &, II III
A GANGSTER'S SYN I II III
THE SAVAGE LIFE I II III
CHAINED TO THE STREETS I II III
BLOOD ON THE MONEY I II
By J-Blunt
PUSH IT TO THE LIMIT
By **Bre' Hayes**
BLOOD OF A BOSS **I, II, III, IV, V**
SHADOWS OF THE GAME
TRAP BASTARD
By **Askari**
THE STREETS BLEED MURDER **I, II & III**
THE HEART OF A GANGSTA I II& III
By **Jerry Jackson**
CUM FOR ME I II III IV V VI
An **LDP Erotica Collaboration**
BRIDE OF A HUSTLA **I II & II**

City of Kingz 2

THE FETTI GIRLS **I, II& III**
CORRUPTED BY A GANGSTA I, II III, IV
BLINDED BY HIS LOVE
THE PRICE YOU PAY FOR LOVE I II
DOPE GIRL MAGIC I II III
By **Destiny Skai**
WHEN A GOOD GIRL GOES BAD
By **Adrienne**
THE COST OF LOYALTY I II III
By Kweli
A GANGSTER'S REVENGE **I II III & IV**
THE BOSS MAN'S DAUGHTERS I II III IV V
A SAVAGE LOVE **I & II**
BAE BELONGS TO ME I II
A HUSTLER'S DECEIT I, II, III
WHAT BAD BITCHES DO I, II, III
SOUL OF A MONSTER I II III
KILL ZONE
A DOPE BOY'S QUEEN I II
By **Aryanna**
A KINGPIN'S AMBITON
A KINGPIN'S AMBITION **II**
I MURDER FOR THE DOUGH
By **Ambitious**
TRUE SAVAGE I II III IV V VI VII
DOPE BOY MAGIC I, II, III

193

Chris Green

MIDNIGHT CARTEL I II III

CITY OF KINGZ I II

By **Chris Green**

A DOPEBOY'S PRAYER

By **Eddie "Wolf" Lee**

THE KING CARTEL **I, II & III**

By **Frank Gresham**

THESE NIGGAS AIN'T LOYAL **I, II & III**

By **Nikki Tee**

GANGSTA SHYT **I II &III**

By **CATO**

THE ULTIMATE BETRAYAL

By **Phoenix**

BOSS'N UP **I , II & III**

By **Royal Nicole**

I LOVE YOU TO DEATH

By Destiny J

I RIDE FOR MY HITTA

I STILL RIDE FOR MY HITTA

By **Misty Holt**

LOVE & CHASIN' PAPER

By **Qay Crockett**

TO DIE IN VAIN

SINS OF A HUSTLA

By **ASAD**

BROOKLYN HUSTLAZ

City of Kingz 2

By **Boogsy Morina**
BROOKLYN ON LOCK I & II
By **Sonovia**
GANGSTA CITY
By **Teddy Duke**
A DRUG KING AND HIS DIAMOND I & II III
A DOPEMAN'S RICHES
HER MAN, MINE'S TOO I, II
CASH MONEY HO'S
THE WIFEY I USED TO BE
By **Nicole Goosby**
TRAPHOUSE KING **I II & III**
KINGPIN KILLAZ I II III
STREET KINGS I II
PAID IN BLOOD **I II**
CARTEL KILLAZ I II III
DOPE GODS I II
By **Hood Rich**
LIPSTICK KILLAH **I, II, III**
CRIME OF PASSION I II & III
FRIEND OR FOE I II
By **Mimi**
STEADY MOBBN' **I, II, III**
THE STREETS STAINED MY SOUL
By **Marcellus Allen**
WHO SHOT YA **I, II, III**

Chris Green

SON OF A DOPE FIEND I II
Renta
GORILLAZ IN THE BAY **I II III IV**
TEARS OF A GANGSTA I II
3X KRAZY I II
DE'KARI
TRIGGADALE I II III
Elijah R. Freeman
GOD BLESS THE TRAPPERS I, II, III
THESE SCANDALOUS STREETS I, II, III
FEAR MY GANGSTA I, II, III IV, V
THESE STREETS DON'T LOVE NOBODY I, II
BURY ME A G I, II, III, IV, V
A GANGSTA'S EMPIRE I, II, III, IV
THE DOPEMAN'S BODYGAURD I II
THE REALEST KILLAZ I II III
Tranay Adams
THE STREETS ARE CALLING
Duquie Wilson
MARRIED TO A BOSS... I II III
By Destiny Skai & Chris Green
KINGZ OF THE GAME I II III IV V
Playa Ray
SLAUGHTER GANG I II III
RUTHLESS HEART I II III
By Willie Slaughter

196

FUK SHYT

By Blakk Diamond

DON'T F#CK WITH MY HEART I II

By Linnea

ADDICTED TO THE DRAMA I II III

IN THE ARM OF HIS BOSS II

By Jamila

YAYO I II III IV

A SHOOTER'S AMBITION I II

By S. Allen

TRAP GOD I II III

By Troublesome

FOREVER GANGSTA

GLOCKS ON SATIN SHEETS I II

By Adrian Dulan

TOE TAGZ I II III

LEVELS TO THIS SHYT

By Ah'Million

KINGPIN DREAMS I II

By Paper Boi Rari

CONFESSIONS OF A GANGSTA I II III

By Nicholas Lock

I'M NOTHING WITHOUT HIS LOVE

SINS OF A THUG

By Monet Dragun

CAUGHT UP IN THE LIFE I II III

Chris Green

City of Kingz 2

By K'ajji
CREAM
By Yolanda Moore
NIGHTMARES OF A HUSTLA I II
By King Dream
CONCRETE KILLAZ
By Kingpen
HARD AND RUTHLESS
By Von Wiley Hall
GHOST MOB II
Stilloan Robinson
MOB TIES
By SayNoMore
BODYMORE MURDERLAND
By Delmont Player

BOOKS BY LDP'S CEO, CA$H

TRUST IN NO MAN

TRUST IN NO MAN 2

TRUST IN NO MAN 3

BONDED BY BLOOD

SHORTY GOT A THUG

THUGS CRY

THUGS CRY 2

THUGS CRY 3

TRUST NO BITCH

TRUST NO BITCH 2

TRUST NO BITCH 3

TIL MY CASKET DROPS

RESTRAINING ORDER

RESTRAINING ORDER 2

IN LOVE WITH A CONVICT

LIFE OF A HOOD STAR

City of Kingz 2